Marcel Proust was born in Paris in 1871 and spent his youth amongst the fashionable and wealthy denizens of French high society, whose foibles he was later to immortalize in his masterpiece *Remembrance of Things Past*. *Pleasures and Regrets*, his earliest work, was first published in 1896. Marcel Proust died in 1922.

By the same author

Remembrance of Things Past
Jean Santeuil

MARCEL PROUST

Pleasures and Regrets

Translated from the French by Louise Varese

With a Preface by D. J. Enright

CHARTERHOUSE LIBRARY

WITHDRAWN

GRAFTON BOOKS

A Division of the Collins Publishing Group

LONDON GLASGOW
TORONTO SYDNEY AUCKLAND

Grafton Books
A Division of the Collins Publishing Group
8 Grafton Street, London W1X 3LA

Published by Grafton Books 1988

This edition first published in Great Britain by
Peter Owen Publishers Ltd 1986

Translation copyright © Lear Publishers, Inc 1948
Translation copyright © renewed Crown Publishers Inc 1976
Preface to this edition © Peter Owen Ltd 1986

ISBN 0-586-07146-6

Printed and bound in Great Britain by
Collins, Glasgow

Set in Baskerville

All rights reserved. No part of this publication
may be reproduced, stored in a retrieval system,
or transmitted, in any form, or by any means,
electronic, mechanical, photocopying, recording or
otherwise, without the prior permission of
the publishers.

This book is sold subject to the condition that
it shall not, by way of trade or otherwise, be
lent, re-sold, hired out or otherwise circulated
without the publisher's prior consent in any
form of binding or cover other than that
in which it is published and without a similar
condition including this condition being
imposed on the subsequent purchaser.

Contents

Preface

Les Plaisirs et les Jours. . . . Was it modesty or cynicism that led Marcel Proust to adapt Hesiod's title *Works and Days* for his first book by substituting Pleasures for Works? Probably neither, but simply a casual, amused sense of fitness.

Published in 1896, when he was twenty-five, this collection of stories and sketches strikes us as very much a product of its age, with its mixture of decadent romanticism and unromantic "realism", of seeming simplicity and conscious sophistication, and its hints of inexpressible wickedness. What exactly were the depravities into which the heroine of "A Young Girl's Confession" was initiated in her sixteenth year? What form did her "sinful pleasures" take? And yet today, when every variety of love shouts its name, we ought to feel gratified that such things are left to our imagination.

In his preface to the first edition Anatole France put it rather well, not only in a characteristically *fin-de-siècle* manner, combining the frigid with the overheated, but actually adumbrating a definition of that manner: the book, he wrote, was "young with the youth of its author" but "old with the age of the world". Whether this served as an effective piece of promotion is doubtful, especially in view of the succeeding references to the book's air of fatigue (albeit noble and beautiful), its hot-house atmosphere, and its "sophisticated orchids whose strange and morbid

beauty is not nourished in the earth". The young Proust
emerges from this encomium sounding like a cross between
Oscar Wilde at his most affected and Walter Pater's vision
of the Mona Lisa. There was, as Arnold observed of Keats,
flint and iron in him, qualities that are discernible even in
these elegant and slightly overripe first fruits.

When in a letter Proust alluded to *Pleasures and Regrets* as
"this flowery book" he surely had in mind the illustrations
to the original and de-luxe edition provided by Madeleine
Lemaire (1845–1928), of whom Dumas *fils* remarked, "No
one, except God, has created more roses." This none too
talented painter was a fashionable society hostess—George
D. Painter records that the streets around her house were
blocked by carriages whenever she gave a reception—and
is thought to have contributed to Proust's Mme Verdurin,
whose salon features throughout *Remembrance of Things
Past*. Even so, the young Proust's style is at times flowery
itself, and not only with flowers of evil. The account of the
Tuileries garden, with its talk of the sun falling asleep on
each of the stone steps one after another like some lightly
slumbering blond boy, is a full-blooded example of the
would-be sublime at once collapsing into the ridiculously
precious. Yet some of the descriptions of landscape, sky and
sea anticipate the great set pieces in *Remembrance of Things
Past*, and even that same passage comes near to redeeming
itself in its picture of the stone horseman blowing his
trumpet without cease against the black sky.

The author is a little too intent on showing the ease with
which he writes, as though exertion, even if only faintly to
be suspected, were a sign of ill breeding and inspiration
virtually the whole of genius. He is keen to preserve his

amateur status, at least for a while yet. And his attack on snobbery may impress us as itself snobbish: the truly "distinguished" figure, the person properly to be admired in society, will be careful not to betray the signs, observed in unsuccessful snobs, of social insecurity. The species of snobbery to which he objects implies that there are people to whom one is inferior, and to equal whom one is willing to sacrifice a great deal indeed—friendships, loves, freedom of thought, duties, dignity, money, time, according to one of the "Fragments from Italian Comedy". The sheer exertion involved in making such sacrifices is equally vulgar, and not to be detected in the higher snobbery!

Talking of ease, it is easy enough for us today to recognize signs and portents of the greater work to come, one which, incidentally, required immense exertions, devotion and self-discipline. Painter comments that the stories are "reservoirs of Time Lost", a vat from which their rudimentary characters will eventually emerge as the developed and shaped flesh-and-blood figures of *Remembrance of Things Past*. Characteristic themes too are sounded—time, jealousy, loss, regret, force of habit—which are to reappear with all their proliferating variations about them.

Another of the "Fragments from Italian Comedy" describes the tyranny of polite society, the way it imposes set roles on its members. A fat woman is benevolent because, being fat, she cannot possibly be malicious; one man is labelled as a wit who would sacrifice his best friend for the sake of an epigram; another has deplorable vices but is faithful and affectionate; a third man is frank to the point of outright rudeness, but "everyone knows" that beneath lies a quivering sensibility. So potent are these attributions, these "ready-made characters", that the fat woman can spread scandal with impunity, the faithful friend can betray his acquaintances and cast off his relatives, the frank individual can go round being heartlessly impertinent. . . . It will make no difference to their reputations, for society knows best.

More gently Proust points out that, despite the theory that whom the Lord or whoever it may be loveth he chasteneth, frankness is often the outpouring of ill humour, and flattery sometimes the overflowing of tenderness. His psychology is less adolescent than his prose style; harsh and sad it can be, but there is no weariness of the eyelids about it.

Violante—Proust's proper names tend to lushness at this stage—is a lover of solitude and meditation, plainly superior to the *beau monde* into which she has moved temporarily, for a vacation as it were. Though she soon conquers that world and fails to find satisfaction in it, though it denies the needs of her imagination and offends her deeper instincts, she will never return to her home in the country, the lost paradise. Force of habit, in the absence of a guiding will and in the presence of an otherwise harmless tinge of vanity, overcomes disgust, contempt and even boredom. Habit, says Proust in *The Guermantes Way*, is "of all the plants of human growth, the one that has least need of nutritious soil in order to live",* and he observes in *The Captive* that "the regularity of a habit is usually in direct proportion to its absurdity".

*Quotations from *Remembrance of Things Past* are taken from the translation by C.K. Scott Moncrieff and Terence Kilmartin, published in 1981.

The end of jealousy, in the story of that name, comes only with the end of life, or a little before. Honoré has much less reason for his jealousy than do Swann and Saint-Loup and Marcel, but for him, as for them, it is comparable to a physical pain but worse, since (as *Remembrance of Things Past* has it) "to determine not to think of it was to think of it still", and it assumes the hideously "noble" guise of a passion for truth, for knowing the truth in all its detail. The jealous person is "like a historian who has to write the history of a period for which he has no documents".

The love that is investigated, sketchily yet painfully, in the precocious parables of *Pleasures and Regrets* is perverse as distinct—for Proust's famous habit of transposing male lovers with female is irrelevant—from perverted. We may want to berate his characters when they throw themselves in the way of misery, or give them a good shaking, but it cannot be denied that perversity is a human trait that dates back to just before the Fall. Mme de Breyves conceives an overriding passion for someone whom she has seen only once, who is utterly nondescript; since there is no reason in her love, there can be no remedy for it. (We think of Swann's discovery, when his love for Odette has ended, that he has wasted years of his life for a woman who wasn't even his type.) The man's potency in her mind rests on his physical absence; and the shrewd comment is made that he would be astonished to learn of the enhanced existence "he" leads in her imagination.

The idea, with a different stress and in a different context, recurs in section VI of "Regrets, Reveries, Changing Skies": infatuation suffers diminution in the presence of the beloved. In *The Fugitive* Marcel reflects, after Albertine's death, that a great part of the thoughts which form what we call love comes to us while the beloved is away from our side, and so one acquires the habit of musing on an absent person: "Hence death does not make any great difference." In a similarly perverse spirit, section XII suggests that, rather than to those who have made us happy, we should be grateful to those who have caused us suffering, for in devastating our heart and laying it bare they enable us to see plainly and to judge. Suffering brings detachment, which in turn allows the voice of duty and of truth to be heard. Preparing to write his book, Marcel tells himself, "The happy years are the lost, the wasted years, one must wait for suffering before one can work."

A less favourable view of suffering is presented by "A Young Girl's Confession", in which the much-loved mother dies of a heart attack after glimpsing her daughter in a lustful embrace at the window. It has been noted that this looks forward both to Marcel's closeness to his mother and to the pain Mlle Vinteuil's reputation causes her father and the incident in which she embraces her lesbian lover in front of his photograph. So far as I remember, there is no suggestion that the music of M. Vinteuil, regarded as the greatest composer of his time, was enhanced by this suffering.

It is wrong to suppose that *Pleasures and Regrets* is interesting only for its prefigurements of *Remembrance of Things Past*, or as the otherwise negligible juvenilia of someone who later achieved fame. André Maurois's characterization of it—"this perfunctory, over-ornamented, inexpert, and charming volume"—brings together an odd assortment of adjectives. Perfunctory much of it must seem when compared with the exhaustiveness of the great novel, and at times, I have suggested, it seems deliberately negligent and dilettante. Some passages are certainly over-ornamented, while others affect us as almost shockingly bleak. Inexpert? Well, at present the writer rests content with epithets that come readily to hand, and his sentences are of average length, not yet the long rhythmic undulations and intricacies of continuous thought. And only in its more vapid moments does the book deserve to be called charming.

The anecdote related in section VI of "Regrets, Reveries, Changing Skies", hovering between black comedy and pure pathos, anticipates Marcel's relations with Albertine, but is as striking and exemplary as anything in *Remembrance of Things Past*, and more economically managed. "The Death of Baldassare Silvande" is a moving story, neither over-ornamented nor perfunctory, and almost as fine in its last pages as the death scene in Lampedusa's *The Leopard*: "He remembered *Robinson Crusoe*, and evenings in the garden when his sister sang. . . . He thought he was kissing his old nurse, holding his first violin." And whatever its junior relationship to themes in *Remembrance of Things Past*, "The End of Jealousy" is impressive in itself, with another good death scene, and in a different way: without being sentimental it is more humane.

It is generally later in his career that a writer comes to realize how comic touches are far from irreconcilable with profundity and sensitivity, how indeed they can transform the merely earnest into the truly serious, the moribund allegory into the living truth. Comedy is in short supply in *Pleasures and Regrets*, but the parody or pastiche of

Flaubert's Bouvard and Pécuchet has some ironic humour to offer, notably in its account of the artistic tastes and preferences artificially constructed by the couple. Reynaldo Hahn is Teutonic in his surname but Southern by virtue of his Christian name, and thus either to be condemned through the association with Wagner or pardoned in view of Verdi.

As for the women, beautiful and intelligent or beautiful and witless, scattered through the book, I suppose they might be spurned as sex objects of the nineties—"she makes one think of a bird dreaming on one elegant and slender leg", "your arms—arms just sufficiently discouraged to remain simple and charming"—but all the same they are observed with a loving (if unsentimental) care and an exquisite detail rarely accorded to any modern woman, in fiction or outside it. Proust's gift for analysis must have been bestowed at birth.

While deriving quiet amusement from the period flavour of *Pleasures and Regrets* and the world-weary smiles and sighs of an exceptional greenery-yallery young man, we can enjoy the free if at times careless and none too cleanly play of the talents that would later conglomerate into a massive genius, dedicated to precision, nuance and plenitude.

D.J. Enright

Pleasures
AND
Regrets

The Death of Baldassare Silvande
Viscount of Sylvania

"The poets say that Apollo tended the flocks of Admetus; so too, each man is a God in disguise who plays the fool."
—EMERSON

I

"MASTER ALEXIS, don't cry like that. Perhaps your uncle, the Viscount, will give you a horse."

"A big horse, Beppo, or a pony?"

"Perhaps a big horse like M. de Cardenio's. But you mustn't cry like that . . . on your thirteenth birthday!"

The hope of being given a horse and the recollection that he was thirteen years old made Alexis' eyes shine through his tears. But it was not enough to console him altogether, for he still must go to see his uncle, Baldassare Silvande, Viscount of Sylvania. It is true that since the day he had heard people saying that his uncle's malady was incurable he had seen him several times. Only everything was now changed, because Baldassare had learned the nature of his illness and knew that he had only three years, at the most, to live. Moreover, unable to understand how the anguish of this knowledge had not killed his uncle or driven him mad, Alexis felt sure that at the sight of him his own grief would be unbearable. Convinced that his uncle would speak to him of his approaching end, he was afraid he would never be able to hold back his sobs, much less console him. He had always adored his uncle, the biggest, the handsomest, the youngest, the gayest of his relatives. He liked his gray eyes, his blond moustache and, when a little chap, that mysterious and delightful haven of pleasure and of refuge, his knees, as inaccessible as a citadel, as amusing as a merry-go-round, and more inviolable than a temple. Alexis, who highly disapproved of his father's severe and somber way of dressing and who dreamed of a future when, always on horseback, he would be as elegant as a fine lady and splendid as a king, looked upon Baldassare as the highest ideal imaginable for a man. He knew that his uncle was handsome, knew that he, Alexis, resembled him; knew that he was intelligent, generous, and as powerful as a bishop or a general. But he had also learned from his parents' criticisms that the Viscount had faults. He even remembered the violence of his uncle's anger the day his cousin Jean Galeas had laughed at him, remembered how his sparkling eyes had betrayed his satisfied vanity when the Duke of Parma had sent to offer him his sister's hand in marriage (he had, on that occasion, in trying to dissimulate his pleasure, set his jaw and made that habitual grimace

Alexis hated so) , and how contemptuously he always spoke of Lucretia who frankly admitted not liking his music.

Often his parents would allude to other things about his uncle which Alexis did not understand, but which he heard severely censured.

But all Baldassare's faults, even his vulgar grimace, must certainly have disappeared. When his uncle had learned that in two years he would probably be dead, how unimportant all his cousin's mockery, the friendship of the Duke of Parma and his own music must have become for him. Alexis imagined him just as handsome, but solemn now, and even more perfect than before. Yes, solemn and already not altogether of this world. He now felt, mingling with his despair, a little uneasiness and even terror.

The horses had been waiting for a long time. They would have to leave. He climbed into the carriage, then jumped down again to run back to ask his tutor a last piece of advice. His face flushed as he spoke.

"Monsieur Legrand, would it be better if my uncle knew or did not know that I know he is going to die?"

"He must not know, Alexis."

"But if he talks to me about it?"

"He won't talk about it."

"He won't talk about it?" said Alexis, astonished, for this was the only alternative he had not foreseen. Whenever he had tried to imagine the visit to his uncle, he had heard him speaking of death with the gentle gravity of a priest.

"But just supposing he does talk about it?"

"You will say he is mistaken."

"And if I cry?"

"You have already cried too much this morning; you will not cry at your uncle's."

"I won't cry!" exclaimed Alexis in despair. "But then he'll think I'm not unhappy, that I don't love him . . . my darling little uncle!"

And he burst into tears. His mother grew impatient waiting and came to fetch him. They drove away.

After Alexis had handed his little overcoat to the valet in green and white livery with the Sylvania arms, who met them in the hall, he paused a moment with his mother to listen to the sound of a violin coming from a nearby room. Then they were shown into an immense circular room entirely enclosed in glass where his uncle spent the greater part of his time. Opposite the door, on entering, one looked out over the sea and, turning the head a little, over lawns, pastures and woods. At the far end of the room were two cats, roses, poppies and many musical instruments. They waited a moment.

Alexis threw himself into his mother's arms. She thought he wanted to kiss her but he only whispered, his mouth glued to her ear, "How old is my uncle?"

"He will be thirty-six in June."

He wanted to ask, "Do you think he will ever be thirty-six?" but did not dare.

A door opened; Alexis trembled; a servant said, "The Viscount will be with you directly."

Soon the servant returned with two peacocks and a kid which the Viscount took with him everywhere. Then more steps and the door opened again.

"It's nothing," said Alexis, whose heart pounded every time he heard a sound. "It's probably another servant, yes, it must be a servant." But at the same time he heard a gentle voice saying, "Good-day, my little Alexis, and happy birthday."

And when his uncle kissed him he felt frightened. Noticing this, no doubt, his uncle, in order to give him time to recover himself, and without paying any further attention to him, began talking gaily to Alexis' mother, his sister-in-law, who, since the death of his mother, was the person he loved best in the world.

Now Alexis, his courage restored, felt only an immense affection for this young man, still so charming, only a little paler, heroic to the point of simulating gaiety in these tragic moments. He wanted to throw his arms around his uncle's neck but, fearing to weaken his courage and make him lose his admirable control, he did not dare. More than anything else the sad, sweet expression of his uncle's eyes made him want to cry. Alexis knew that his eyes had always been sad and even in his happiest moments seemed to be asking consolation for the sorrows which, to all appearances, did not touch him. But now Alexis believed that all his uncle's sadness, so courageously banished from his conversation, had taken refuge in his eyes, the only things about him, with his emaciated cheeks, that were sincere.

"I know that you would like to drive a carriage and pair, my little Alexis," said Baldassare. "A horse will be brought to you tomorrow. Next year I shall complete the pair, and in two years I shall give you the carriage. But perhaps this year you will learn to ride. We'll try it on my return. For," he added, "I have decided to leave tomorrow, but only for a short time. In a month I shall be back and then, you know, we are going to the matinée together to see that comedy as I promised you."

Alexis knew that his uncle was going to spend several weeks with friends, he also knew that his uncle was still allowed to go to the theatre; but obsessed by the idea of death that had so shattered him before coming to his uncle's, these words caused him a profound and painful astonishment.

"I shan't go," he said to himself. "How all the actors' jokes and the laughter of the audience would make him suffer!"

"What was that charming melody I heard you playing when we came in?" Alexis' mother asked.

"Ah! You liked it?" said Baldassare quickly, with a pleased air. "It is that *Romanza* I was telling you about."

"Is he acting?" wondered Alexis. "How can he care about the success of his music now?"

At this moment the Viscount's face took on an

expression of extreme pain; his cheeks had grown pale, he frowned and bit his lips, his eyes filled with tears.

"Oh, God!" cried Alexis to himself. "This part he is playing is too much for him. My poor uncle! But why is he so afraid of hurting us? Why does he try so hard to control himself?"

But the pains of general paralysis, which at times constricted him as in an iron corset, even leaving the marks of blows on his body, and which just now had been so severe as to contract his face in spite of all his efforts, now disappeared.

Wiping his eyes, he cheerfully resumed the conversation.

"It seems to me the Duke of Parma has been less attentive to you lately," Alexis' mother tactlessly remarked.

"Less attentive!" cried Baldassare, furious. "The Duke of Parma less attentive! But what can you be thinking of? Only this morning he wrote me putting his castle of Illyrie at my disposal, if I thought the mountain air would do me any good."

He got up quickly, but his atrocious pains being brought on again by this sudden movement, he was forced to pause. The minute they had left him he called to his servant, "Bring me that letter by my bed."

And he read it excitedly: "My dear Baldassare, how I miss you and long to see you, etc. etc."

And as the Prince's affability increased during the

course of the letter, Baldassare's face softened and his eyes shone with happy satisfaction. All at once, anxious to disguise his delight which did not seem to him very exalted, he clenched his teeth and made the charming little vulgar grimace that Alexis had supposed forever banished from a face touched by the peace of death.

Seeing this little grimace distorting Baldassare's lips as usual, the scales fell from Alexis' eyes. Ever since he had been with his uncle he had believed, had wanted to believe, he was looking at the face of a dying man forever detached from the vulgar realities of life and that, except for a smile of heroic restraint, sadly tender, celestial and disillusioned, nothing could henceforth disturb its expression of perfect serenity. Now he could no longer doubt that if Jean Galeas were to tease his uncle, it would put him in the same fury as before, that there entered into the sick man's gaiety, his desire to go to the theatre, not the least dissimulation nor any courage, and that having come so near to death, Baldassare continued only to think of life.

Upon reaching home, Alexis was suddenly struck by the thought that he too would some day die, that although he still had a great deal more time before him than his uncle, certainly neither Baldassare's old gardener, nor his cousin, the Duchess d'Aleriouvres, would long survive him. Yet Rocco, rich enough to retire, still worked ceaselessly and was determined to win a prize for his roses. The Duchess, in spite of her seventy years, kept her hair carefully dyed and paid for articles in the papers praising the youthfulness of her step, the elegance of her receptions, the distinction of her table and her mind.

These examples in no way mitigated the startled surprise Alexis had felt at his uncle's attitude, but only inspired in him a kindred astonishment that gradually increased to a prodigious stupefaction before the universal scandal of human lives, not excepting his own, that walked toward death backward with eyes turned toward life.

Determined not to imitate such a shocking aberration he decided that, like the ancient prophets of whose glory he had been told, he would retire into the desert with a few of his young friends. He informed his parents of his decision.

Happily, more potent than their derision, life, whose sweet and fortifying milk he had not yet completely drained, held out her breast to dissuade him, and he began to drink again with a joyous avidity, his rich and credulous imagination naively heeding life's remonstrances, which royally made amends for all his disillusionments.

II

"The flesh is sad, alas. . . ."
—STEPHANE MALLARME

THE DAY after Alexis' visit, the Viscount of Sylvania left for the neighboring château where he was to spend three or four weeks, and where the presence of numerous guests might happily tend to dispel the depression which often followed one of his attacks.

Soon all the pleasures of the place became concentrated in the presence of a young woman who seemed to magnify them for him in sharing them. He felt that she was beginning to be attracted to him but, knowing her to be absolutely virtuous and awaiting with impatience the arrival of her husband, he still kept a certain reserve. Moreover, he was not at all certain of his own feelings and vaguely realized what a sin it would be for him to encourage her in wrongdoing. At what moment the nature of their relations began to alter he could never remember. But, as by a tacit agreement, at some fortuitous moment, he had kissed her wrists, his fingers had fondled her neck. She seemed so happy that one evening he went further: he began by kissing her; then caressed her for a long time and again kissed her eyes, her cheeks, her lips, her neck, the corners of her nose. The young woman's smiling mouth advanced to meet his caresses, and her eyes, in their depths, shone like pools warmed by the sun. Baldassare's caresses grew bolder. At a certain moment he looked at her and was struck by the pallor and the infinite despair her death-like forehead seemed to reveal; her afflicted and weary eyes wept looks much sadder than tears, like the torture endured in crucifixion, or at the loss of someone dearly beloved. He gazed at her for a moment, and she, with a supreme effort, raised toward him her supplicating eyes that begged for grace while her avid mouth, in a convulsive and unconscious movement, still begged for kisses.

And once more overwhelmed, both of them, by the pleasure still floating in the perfume of their kisses, and by the recollection of their caresses, with one accord, they threw themselves upon each other, but henceforth closing their eyes, those cruel eyes which revealed to them their souls' distress. They would not look at their souls, and he especially closed his with all his might, like an executioner overcome by remorse, who feels that his arm will tremble at the moment of striking his victim if, instead of imagining him roused to fury and satisfying his criminal urge, he should look into his face and feel a moment of compassion.

The night had come and she was still in his room, with dry and dreamy eyes. She left him without a word, only kissing his hand with passionate tenderness.

He, however, could not sleep, and if for a moment he dozed off, he would wake with a start, feeling the supplicating and desperate eyes of his victim raised toward his. All at once he imagined her as she must be at the moment, sleepless like him and feeling so utterly alone. He dressed, walked softly to her room, afraid to make a sound for fear of waking her if she slept, afraid to return to his own room where the sky, the earth and his own soul would smother him under their weight. He stayed there outside the young

woman's door, feeling that it would be impossible to
resist another moment, that he must go in; then horrified at the thought of disturbing this sweet oblivion,
for he could perceive the gentle rhythm of her sleeping breath, and of cruelly delivering her over to remorse and despair now that, having escaped their
clutches, she had found an instant's peace, he remained outside her door, sitting or kneeling or sometimes lying down. In the morning he went back to his
room chilled and calm, slept for a long time, and
awoke with a sensation of well-being.

Exerting all their ingenuity to pacify their con-
sciences, they grew accustomed to their remorse, to
their pleasures too, which also became less keen, and
when he returned to Sylvania, he took back with him,
as she did too, only a sweet and somewhat cold memory of those flaming and cruel moments.

III

"His youth makes a noise for him to hear; he does not hear."
—MADAME DE SEVIGNE

WHEN Alexis, on his fourteenth birthday, went to see
his Uncle Baldassare, he did not, as he had expected,
feel any of the violent emotions of the preceding year.
His endless rides on the horse his uncle had given
him, while developing his strength, had dissipated all
his morbid susceptibility and quickened that continuous sensation of perfect health that youth enjoys,

like an obscure consciousness of the depths of its resources and the power of its joyous alacrity. Feeling his chest swelling like a sail in the breeze awakened by his galloping, his body burning like a fire in winter, and his forehead cool as the fugitive branches that whipped him as he rode by, and later, when he returned, the glow of his body under the cold shower or its languorous relish during the savoury pleasures of digestion, he would glory in all this power of life within him which, after having been the tumultuous pride of Baldassare, had left him now forever to rejoice younger souls whom it would in turn one day desert.

Nothing in Alexis could any longer succumb to his uncle's weakness, die at his approaching death. The joyful murmur of the blood in his veins, the desires in his brain, prevented him from hearing the sick man's feeble complaints. Alexis had entered on that ardent period when the body works so vigorously erecting castles between itself and its soul that soon the latter seems to have disappeared, until the day when sickness or sorrow having slowly and painfully undermined those barriers, at the end of the fissure they have opened, *it* reappears. He had grown used to his uncle's mortal illness, as we get used to everything that continues around us unchanged, and although still alive, because he had once made him cry as we cry for the dead, Alexis behaved toward him as we behave toward the dead: he began to forget him.

When his uncle said to him that day: "My little Alexis, I am going to give you the carriage at the same time as the second horse," he understood that his uncle had thought: "Because otherwise you are in danger of never having the carriage at all"; and he knew that this was an extremely sad thought but without *feeling* that it was sad, because actually there was no room in him for profound sadness.

A few days later he was struck by the description in one of his books of a villain who remained unmoved by the heartbreaking tenderness of a dying man who adored him.

When night came, the fear that he was that villain in whom he seemed to recognize himself kept him from sleeping. The next day he took an exhilarating ride on his horse, worked well, felt such tender affection for his living parents that he was soon enjoying himself without scruple and sleeping without remorse.

Meanwhile the Viscount of Sylvania, who was now almost unable to walk, never left the château. Friends and relatives came to see him every day, and he might admit the most reprehensible folly, confess the most absurd extravagances, indulge in paradoxes or reveal the most shocking fault without his relatives ever offering the least reproach, without his friends permitting themselves a pleasantry or contradiction. It seemed as though they had tacitly absolved him of all responsibility for his actions and his words. It seemed, above all, that they were trying to keep him from hearing, as though muffling with gentleness if they could not conquer with caresses, the last creakings of his body that life was leaving.

Lying on his couch he spent long and charming hours tête-à-tête with himself, the only guest he had neglected to invite to supper during his lifetime. He took a melancholy joy in adorning his afflicted body, in nursing his resignation on the vast view of the sea from his windows. With pictures from this world which still filled his mind, but which his gradual departure in already detaching him from them had rendered more beautiful and vague, he surrounded the scene of his death, projected long ago but, like a work of art, ceaselessly retouched with ardent sadness.

In his imagination he had already sketched his farewell scene with Oliviane, his cherished but platonic friend over whose drawing room he had reigned, even when the greatest noblemen, the most glorious artists and wits of Europe were assembled there. He seemed already to be reading the account of their last meeting:

". . . The sun was setting and the sea, visible through the apple boughs, was mauve. Light as light faded garlands and persistent as regrets, little pink and blue clouds floated on the horizon. A melancholy row of poplars was plunged in shadow, the resigned heads in a churchly rose; the last rays of the sun, without touching their trunks, tinted the branches, hanging garlands of light on these balustrades of shade.

The breeze mingled the three odors of sea, wet leaves and milk. Never had the landscape of Sylvania more voluptuously tempered the melancholy of the evening.

" 'I have loved you much, my poor friend, but I have given you little,' she said to him.

" 'How can you say that, Oliviane? You have given me all the more in that I asked for less, and much more, in truth, than if the senses had played a part in our affection. Supernatural as a Madonna, gentle as a nurse, I have adored you and you have cradled me. I loved you with a tenderness whose delicate sagacity no carnal pleasure ever spoiled. And in exchange have you not brought me an incomparable friendship, such lovely tea, a conversation by nature richly graced and how many fragrant roses! You alone, with your maternal and expressive hands, knew how to soothe my fevered brow, drop honey between my parched lips, fill my life with noble images.

" 'Dear friend, give me your hands that I may kiss them.' "

Only the indifference of Pia, the little Syracusian princess whom he still loved with all his senses and his heart and who had herself been smitten by an invincible and furious passion for Castruccio, brought him back from time to time to a more cruel reality, but which he forced himself to disregard. Until only recently he had gone at times to entertainments where strolling with her on his arm he thought to humiliate his rival; but he felt even while she was walking by his side that her eyes were distracted by another love which only her pity for his mortal illness made her try to hide. And now even that was no longer possible. The incoherent movement of his limbs had become such that he could no longer leave the house. But she came to see him often, and as though she had entered into the conspiracy of kindness with the others, spoke to him with an ingenious tenderness never, as formerly, contradicted by an exclamation of anger or admission of indifference. And more than that of any of the others he felt the solace of her kindness spread over him and ravish him.

But then one day, rising from his chair to go to table, his astonished servant saw him walking almost steadily. He sent for the doctor, who reversed his verdict. The next day he walked normally. At the end of a week he was permitted to go out. His relatives and friends now began to entertain hopes for his recovery. The doctor wondered if possibly a simple and curable nervous malady had at first taken on the symptoms of general paralysis, which now effectively began to disappear. To Baldassare he presented his conjectures as a certainty: "You are saved!"

The condemned man was visibly overjoyed by his reprieve. But at the end of a certain time, improvement having continued, a sharp uneasiness began to pierce through his joy which habit, even in so short a time, had begun to weaken. Sheltered from all the inclemencies of life in that propitious atmosphere of ambient sweetness, of enforced calm and free meditation, obscurely the desire for death began to germinate in him. He was still far from suspecting the truth, and felt only a vague dread at the thought of beginning life again, of suffering all its blows to which he had grown unaccustomed, and of forfeiting the tenderness with which he had been surrounded. He also vaguely felt that it would be wrong to lose himself in pleasure and in action again, now that he had made the acquaintance of his other self, of that fraternal stranger with whom, so remote and yet so close, he had conversed for hours as he watched the boats ploughing through the sea. And as though he felt a new natal love, before unknown, awake in him, like a young man who has all his life been mistaken about the country of his birth, he felt homesick for death which, at first, had seemed to him a land of eternal exile.

One day when he expressed a certain idea, Jean Galeas, who knew that he was cured, contradicted him violently and ironically. His sister-in-law, who for the last two months had visited him every morning and evening, now let two days go by without coming to see him. That was too much! For so long a stranger to life's rhythm, he was loath to re-adapt himself to it now. But only because he had not yet been caught again by all its charm. Even his strength returned and with it his desire for life. He went out,

began to live again and died a second time to his own
self. At the end of a month the symptoms of general
paralysis reappeared. Little by little, as before, walking became difficult, impossible, but so gradually that
he had time to grow used to his return to death and
to turn his head the other way. The relapse did not
even have the virtue of the first attack which, toward
the end, had begun to make him feel detached from
life so that he saw it, not yet in its reality, but as
though looking at a picture. Now, on the contrary, he
grew more and more vain, irascible, feverishly regret-
ting the pleasures he could no longer enjoy.

His sister-in-law, coming several times a day with
Alexis, alone brought a little sweetness to his last days.

One afternoon, when she was on her way to the
Viscount's, within a short distance of his house the
horses suddenly took fright. She was thrown violently
out of the carriage, trampled by a passing horseman,
and carried unconscious to Baldassare's with a frac-
tured skull.

The coachman who had escaped injury came at
once to announce the accident to the Viscount, whose
face turned livid at the news. He ground his teeth,
his shining eyes almost started from their sockets and
in a frightful access of rage he began inveighing
against the coachman interminably. But it seemed as
though these bursts of violence were trying to hide a
cry of pain which at intervals could be faintly heard.
It was as though a sick person were groaning near the

infuriated man. Soon this moaning, feeble at first, finally smothered his cries of rage, and he sank sobbing into a chair.

Then he wanted them to wash his face for fear the sight of the traces of his grief might distress his sister-in-law. The servant sadly shook his head, the injured woman had not regained consciousness. Two days and nights Baldassare watched in agony beside his sister-in-law's bed. She might die at any moment. The second night a dangerous operation was undertaken. On the morning of the third day the fever broke and the sick woman looked at Baldassare and smiled. He could not keep back his tears and wept for joy without stopping. When, little by little, death had crept toward him he had refused to face it; now suddenly he found himself in its presence. It had horrified him by threatening what was dearest to him in life. He had begged for mercy. It had yielded.

He felt himself strong and free, proud to discover that his own life was less precious to him than that of his sister-in-law, and that he had felt as much contempt for the one as compassion for the other. It was death now he looked at, face to face, and not the imagined settings of his own death. He longed to remain like this until the end, no longer the dupe of his own fabrications which, by creating a magnificent and memorable end, would have been the final profanation sullying the mysteries of his death as it had robbed him of the mysteries of his life.

──────────────────── IV ────────────────────

"Tomorrow, and tomorrow, and tomorrow,
Creeps in this petty pace from day to day,
To the last syllable of recorded time;
And all our yesterdays have lighted fools
The way to dusty death. Out, out, brief candle!
Life's but a walking shadow; a poor player,
That struts and frets his hour upon the stage,
And then is heard no more: it is a tale
Told by an idiot, full of sound and fury,
Signifying nothing.—"

—SHAKESPEARE: *Macbeth*

ALL the emotions, the fatigues Baldassare had suffered during his sister-in-law's illness had accelerated the course of his own. He had just been told by his confessor that he had only a month more to live; it was ten o'clock in the morning, it was raining in torrents. A carriage stopped in front of the château. It was the Duchess Oliviane. Once he had thought to embellish harmoniously his death-bed scenes:

". . . . It will be on some limpid evening. The sun will have set and the sea, visible through the apple boughs, will be mauve. Light as light faded garlands and persistent as regrets, little pink and blue clouds will float on the horizon. . . ."

It was ten o'clock in the morning, under a low murky sky, in a pelting rain, that the Duchess Oliviane arrived. Worn out by his illness, completely absorbed by more exalted thoughts and no longer touched by the charm of things which formerly seemed to him to embody the value, and the grace, and all the delicate glory of life, he had them tell the

Duchess that he was now too weak to see her. And although she still insisted, making them inquire again, he still refused. It was not even from a sense of duty; she simply meant nothing to him any longer. Death had been quick to break the bonds of an enslavement that during the last few weeks he had dreaded. Now as he tried to recall her to mind, nothing appeared to the eyes of his spirit, and those of his imagination and of his vanity were closed.

Yet, about a week before his death, the announcement of a ball to be given by the Duchess of Bohemia where Pia was to lead the cotillion with Castruccio, who was leaving the following day for Denmark, furiously revived his jealousy. He asked to have Pia sent for; his sister-in-law hesitated. He thought they wanted to prevent his seeing her, were willfully tormenting him, and became angry. Not to vex him, they sent for her at once.

When she arrived he was perfectly calm, but profoundly sad. He drew her close to his bed and began immediately talking to her of the ball to be given by the Duchess of Bohemia. He said to her, "As we are not related you will not wear mourning for me. But I want to beg one favor of you. Promise me that you will not go to the ball."

They looked into each other's eyes, and saw their two souls peering from their depths, their melancholy and passionate souls that death had been unable to unite. He understood her hesitation; his lips contracted painfully and he said gently, "No! No! Don't

promise. Don't break a promise to a dying man. If
you are not sure of yourself, you must not promise."

"I cannot promise. I have not seen him for two
months and shall perhaps never see him again. I
should be inconsolable for all eternity if I did not go
to the ball."

"You are right, since you love him . . . and death is
inevitable . . . that you should go on living with all
your might. . . . But you will do one little thing for
me. From the time you would have stayed at the ball
steal just that little which, to arrest suspicion, you
would have had to spend with me. Let my soul remember those few instants with you; for just that moment, think of me."

"I cannot even promise you that much. The ball
will last for such a little while. Even without leaving
him at all, I shall have scarcely enough time to see
him. But I promise that I will give you a moment
every day of all the days to come."

"You cannot, you will forget me. But if after a year,
alas! a little longer perhaps, some sad book, a death,
a rainy evening, makes you think of me, that will be
a kindness! I shall never, never see you again . . . except as a soul, and for that we should have to think of
each other at the same time. I shall never cease to
think of you, so that my soul will be continually open,
ready, if ever it should please you to enter. But how
long the guest will keep me waiting! The rains of
November will have rotted the flowers on my grave,
June will have burned them, and my soul will be

weeping with impatience. Ah! I hope one day the sight of some souvenir, a birthday coming round again, the bent of your thoughts, will bring your memory within the circle of my tenderness. Then it will be as though I had heard you, seen you, as by enchantment flowers had sprung up at your coming. Think of me when I am dead. But, alas! how can I hope that death and your graver mood will accomplish what life with all its ardors, and our tears, our gaieties and lips have failed to do?"

V

"Now cracks a noble heart;—Good night, sweet prince;
And flights of angels sing thee to thy rest!"
—SHAKESPEARE: *Hamlet*

MEANWHILE a fever, accompanied by delirium, never left the Viscount. His bed had been placed in the vast rotunda where Alexis had seen him on his thirteenth birthday, had seen him still so gay, and whence the sick man could look out over the sea and the jetty of the harbor and at the same time on the other side, over the pastures and the woods. From time to time he would talk in his delirium. But his words no longer bore the trace of those thoughts from above which during the last few weeks had purified him by their visits. With violent imprecations against some invisible person who was making fun of him, he kept repeating that he was the greatest musician of the age, the most illustrious nobleman of the whole universe.

Then, suddenly calmed, he would tell his coachman to take him to some low dive, to have the horses saddled for the hunt. He asked for note paper that he might invite all the sovereigns of Europe to a dinner in honor of his marriage to the sister of the Duke of Parma. Terrified at not being able to pay a gambling debt, he caught up a paper knife beside his bed and aimed it like a pistol at his head. He sent to find out whether the policeman he had thrashed the night before had died, and to a person whose hand he thought he was holding, laughingly whispered obscenities. Those destroying angels called Will and Thought were no longer there to drive back into the shadows the evil spirits of his senses and the base emanations of his memory. At the end of three days, toward five o'clock, he awoke as from a bad dream for which one is not responsible but which one vaguely remembers. He asked if any friends or relatives had been present during the time he had revealed only the infamous, the most primitive and the most extinct part of himself, and he begged that if he became delirious again they should immediately leave the room and that no one should be allowed to return until he had regained consciousness.

He let his eyes wander around the room, and smiling watched his black cat, which had climbed onto a Chinese vase, playing with a chrysanthemum with the gesture of a mime smelling a flower. He made everyone leave him and spoke at length with the priest who was attending him. However, he refused to take communion and asked the doctor to say that his stomach could no longer tolerate the host. At the end of an hour he asked that his sister-in-law and Jean Galeas return. He said, "I am resigned, I am happy to die and to appear before God."

The air was so mild that they opened the windows facing the sea but, the wind coming from the other direction, they kept the ones closed that overlooked the pastures and the woods.

Baldassare had his bed moved over to the open windows. A boat which sailors had been pulling along the jetty by a rope, set sail. In the bow a handsome cabin-boy, fifteen years of age perhaps, leaned far out over the water. With every swell it seemed as though he would be thrown into the sea, but he stood firmly on his sturdy legs. In his hands he held a net for drawing in the fish and between his salty lips a lighted pipe. And the same breeze that swelled the sail came in through the open window cooling Baldassare's hot cheeks, and sending a paper fluttering around the room. He turned his head away to shut out the sight of pleasures he had so passionately loved and would never know again. He glanced at the harbor: a three-master was setting sail.

"That ship is leaving for the Indies," said Jean Galeas.

Baldassare could not make out the people standing on the wharf waving their handkerchiefs, but he imagined all the thirst for the unknown altering the expression of their eyes. They had so much more life to live, so much more to learn, to feel. The anchor was weighed, a cry arose, and the boat glided away over the somber sea toward the west where in a golden mist the light, mingling tiny boats and clouds together, murmured vague and irresistible promises to the travelers.

Baldassare had them close the windows on that side of the rotunda and open the ones overlooking the pastures and the woods. He looked at the fields but still heard the cry of farewell that had risen from the three-master, still saw the cabin-boy, his pipe between his teeth, holding out his net.

Baldassare's hand moved feverishly. All at once he heard a little silvery noise, almost imperceptible and as profound as the beating of a heart. It was the sound of bells coming from a distant village, which, thanks to the limpidity of the atmosphere that evening and the propitious breeze, had reached him across leagues of plain and forest and been caught by his faithful ear. It was a very ancient voice and it was the voice of today. And he felt his heart beat to the bells' harmonious flight, inhaling at the moment they seemed to be breathing in the sound, exhaling with them in a feeble long-drawn breath. During his whole life, whenever he heard the sound of distant bells, he always remembered their sweetness on the evening air when as a tiny boy he used to come home to the castle across the fields.

At this moment the doctor beckoned everyone to approach, saying, "This is the end!"

Baldassare lay with closed eyes, and his heart listened to the bells which his ears, paralyzed by approaching death, could no longer hear. Once more he saw his mother kissing him as she always did when he came home, then in the evening tucking him in bed, warming his feet in her hands, staying with him if he could not sleep. He remembered *Robinson Crusoe,* and evenings in the garden when his sister sang, and his professor predicted that one day he would be a great musician, and his mother's emotion which she tried in vain to hide. Now there was no more time to realize that passionate expectation of his mother and sister which he had so cruelly disappointed. He saw again the tall linden tree under which he had become betrothed and the day when his betrothal had been broken when only his mother had known how to comfort him. He thought he was kissing his old nurse, holding his first violin. He saw it all again through a luminous distance, sweet and sad like the one on which the sightless windows gazed, facing woods and pastures.

All this he saw, yet not two minutes had elapsed since the doctor, listening to his heart, had said, "This is the end!" Then, rising, "All is over."

Alexis, his mother, and Jean Galeas knelt down, together with the Duke of Parma, who had just arrived. The servants were weeping in the open doorway.

October, 1894

A Young Girl's Confession

"The cravings of the senses drag us hither and thither, but when the hour is spent, what do you bring back with you? Remorse of conscience and dissipation of the spirit. You go out in joy and in sadness you return, and the pleasures of the evening sadden the morning. Thus the joys of the senses first flatter us, but in the end they wound and kill."
—*Imitation of Jesus Christ, Book I,c.XVIII*

"Through the forgetfulness we seek from counterfeit delights,
Amidst our frenzies comes, more virginal and sweet,
The melancholy scent of lilacs."
—HENRI DE REGNIER

I

AT LAST DELIVERANCE is almost here. Of course I was clumsy. I didn't know how to shoot; I almost missed myself. Of course it would have been better to have died at once, but after all, they were not able to extract the bullet and then heart complications set in.

It cannot be much longer now. And yet—eight days more! It can last another eight days! during which I shall be able to do nothing but reconstruct the horrible chain of events. If I were not so weak, if I had sufficient strength of will to get up, to leave here, I would go to *Les Oublis* to die, in the park where all my summers were spent until I was fifteen. No other place is so full of my mother, so completely has her presence and even more her absence, impregnated it with her being. For to one who loves, is not absence the most effective, the most tenacious, the most indestructible, the most faithful of presences?

My mother would take me to *Les Oublis* toward the end of April, would leave again after two days, spend two more days there in the middle of May, then, in the last week of June would come to take me away. These visits, so short, were the sweetest and the most cruel thing to me. During these two days she would be lavish of her tenderness which habitually, in order to strengthen me and mitigate my excessive susceptibility, she would avariciously withhold. On the two evenings she spent at *Les Oublis*, she would come to kiss me goodnight after I was in bed, an old custom which she had abandoned because it caused me too much pleasure and too much pain, because due to my calling her back to say goodnight again and again I could never go to sleep, not daring finally to call her any more, but feeling more than ever the passionate need, always inventing new excuses, my burning pillow to be turned, my icy feet which her hands alone could warm. Such sweet moments gained an added sweetness from my feeling that during them my mother was her true self and that her habitual reserve must cost her dearly. The day she left, day of despair, when I would cling to her skirts until she got on the train, imploring her to take me with her to Paris, I readily discerned the truth through her dissimulation, sensed her sadness through her gay and irritated reproaches at my "stupid, ridiculous" sadness which she wanted to teach me to dominate but which she shared. I still feel the emotion of a certain day of departure (the identical emotion, intact, unaltered in its painful return today) on which I made the sweet discovery of her tenderness, so similar and so superior to my own. Like all discoveries, I had already sensed, divined it, but it seemed so often in practice to be contradicted! My happiest recollections are of those times when she would be called back to *Les Oublis* when I was ill. Not only was it an extra visit on which I had not counted but, above all, during that time she was all overflowing gentleness and tenderness, undisguised and unrestrained. Even at that time, before they had acquired an added poignancy from the thought that one day they would no longer be there for me, that gentleness and tenderness meant so much to me that the charm of convalescence was always unbearably sad: the day was approaching when I should be sufficiently well again for my mother to leave me, and until then not sufficiently ill to keep her any longer from returning to her former severity and unmitigated justice.

One day my uncles with whom I stayed at *Les Oublis* had kept from me the news that my mother was coming that day, fearing that in the joyful anguish of that expectation, I should neglect a young cousin who had come to visit me for a few hours. That deception was perhaps the first of the circumstances which, independent of my own volition, were the accomplices of all those evil tendencies which, like other children of my age, and no more than they, I bore within me. This young cousin, a boy of fifteen—I was then fourteen—was already very depraved, and told me things which instantly made me shudder with remorse and voluptuousness. Listening to him, letting his hands fondle mine, I tasted a joy poisoned at its very source; soon I found strength enough to leave him, and fled through the park feeling an insane need of my mother whom I knew, alas! to be in Paris, calling to her, in spite of myself, along all the *allées*. Suddenly, as I was running past a vine-covered arbor, I saw her sitting on a bench, smiling and holding out her arms to me. She threw back her veil to kiss me and I flung myself against her cheeks, bursting into tears. I cried for a long time, telling her all those ugly things which it took the ignorance of my youth to be able to confess, and to which, without understanding them, my mother listened divinely, minimizing their importance with a goodness that lightened the weight of my conscience. That weight grew lighter, grew lighter; my crushed and humiliated soul rose more and more buoyant and strong, overflowed—I was all soul. A divine fragrance emanated from my mother and from my recovered innocence. Soon I was conscious of another odor in my nostrils just as fresh and pure. It came from a lilac bush, one of whose branches, hid-

den by my mother's parasol, was already in flower
and unseen was filling the air with its perfume. High
in the trees birds were singing with all their strength.
Higher still, between the green tops, the sky was so
deep a blue that it seemed merely the entrance to a
sky where one could climb forever. I kissed my
mother. Never have I recaptured the sweetness of that
kiss. She left again the following day, and that departure was more cruel than all those that had preceded
it. It seemed to me now, having once sinned, that together with happiness, strength and the necessary suc-
cor were abandoning me.

All these separations taught me, in spite of myself,
what the coming of the irrevocable one would be, although at the time I had never really considered the
possibility of surviving my mother. I had determined
to kill myself the instant following her death. Later,
absence taught me other and still more bitter lessons,
that one grows accustomed to absence, that the greatest diminution of oneself, the most humiliating suffering is to feel that one no longer suffers. These lessons, moreover, were later to be contradicted. I keep
thinking now especially of that little garden where I
used to breakfast with my mother, and where there
were innumerable pansies. They always seemed to me
a little sad, grave as emblems, but soft and velvety,
often mauve, sometimes violet, almost black with
graceful and mysterious yellow images, some altogether white and of a fragile innocence. I gather them

all in memory now, those pansies, their sadness has been increased from having been understood, their velvet softness has forever disappeared.

II

How is it possible that the pure water of these memories, gushing forth again, could flow through my impure soul of today without being defiled? What special virtue has the matinal fragrance of lilacs that is able to pass through such fetid vapors without mingling with them and without losing any of its strength? Alas! although within me, it is yet so far from me—it is outside myself—that my fourteen-year-old soul wakes again. I know well that it is my soul no longer, and that it is no longer within my power to make it mine again. In those days, however, I did not think that I should one day regret its loss. It was but pure, I was to make it strong and capable in the future of the highest tasks. Often at *Les Oublis,* after being with my mother beside waters full of the play of sunlight and fishes during the hottest part of the day—or mornings and evenings, walking with her through the fields, I would dream with confidence of that future which was never fair enough to satisfy her love or my desire to please her, nor the forces, if not of will at least of imagination and of feeling, which stirred in me, tumultuously calling upon the destiny wherein they would be realized, knocking repeatedly against the wall of my heart as though to burst it open and to rush forth into life. If in those days I jumped up and down with all my might, kissed my mother a thousand times, running far ahead of her like a little dog, or lagged behind to pick cornflowers and poppies and brought them to her, shouting, it was not so much for the joy the walk and the gathering of flowers afforded me, as to give vent to my happiness in feeling so much life within me ready to gush forth and spread out infinitely toward perspectives even vaster and more enchanting than the farthermost horizon of forest and sky which I longed to reach at a single bound. O poppies, cornflowers and clover, if I bore you off in such a frenzy, all aquiver and with blazing eyes, if you made me laugh and made me cry, it was because in the bunches that I made of you, all those hopes of mine were tied up too. Hopes which, like you, have dried and withered but which, without ever having flowered like you, have all returned to dust.

What grieved my mother was my lack of will. I did everything on the impulse of the moment. As long as the impulse came from mind or heart my life, while not perfect, was not altogether bad. The realization of all my fine projects for work, for calm and reflection preoccupied my mother and myself above everything else, because we felt, she more clearly, I vaguely but intensely, that it would be nothing more than the image, projected into life, of that will created by myself within myself which my mother had conceived and nurtured. But always I would put it off until to-

morrow. I would give myself time, miserable sometimes to see it passing, but after all, for me there was
still so much ahead! I was a little frightened, nevertheless, and felt vaguely that this habit of getting
along without using my will weighed on me more and
more with the years, sadly suspecting that things
would not change suddenly, that I could scarcely
count on a miracle which would cost me nothing to
change my life and create a will for me. To wish to
possess a will was not enough. What I had to do was
precisely what I could not do without a will: to will
to have one.

——————————— III ———————————

"And concupiscence' furious wind
Set your flesh clacking like an old flag."
—Baudelaire

During my sixteenth year I went through a period
of nervous depression which affected my health. To
divert me my parents had me make my debut. Young
men began to call on me. One of them was depraved
and evil. His manners were, at once, gentle and impudent. He was the one with whom I fell in love. My
parents discovered it but, fearing to hurt me, they
avoided taking any precipitous steps. Spending all the
time I was not with him thinking about him, I finally
sank so low as to resemble him as nearly as that was
possible. He initiated me to depravity almost without
my realizing it, then accustomed me to encourage the

evil thoughts that awoke in me and which I had not
the will to oppose, the only power capable of forcing
them back into the infernal darkness from whence
they came. When love died, habit had taken its place,
and there was no lack of immoral young men to ex-
ploit it. The accomplices of my sins, they made themselves apologists to my conscience as well. At first I
was filled with the most atrocious remorse. I made
confessions which were not understood. My companions dissuaded me from being more explicit with my
father. They convinced me, little by little, that all
girls did the same things and that parents only pre-
tended not to know it. My imagination soon likened
the lies I was forced to tell to silences that must be
kept on some ineluctable necessity. At that time my
way of living was already bad; still I dreamed,
thought, felt.

Seeking to divert my mind from my evil desires and
to drive them away, I began to go more and more into
society. Its withering pleasures accustomed me to living perpetually in company, and I lost, with my taste
for solitude, the secret of those joys which, until now,
nature and art had given me. Never had I gone to
concerts as often as during those years. Never, entirely preoccupied as I was with the desire of being
admired in some fashionable box, did I feel the music
less profoundly. I listened and heard nothing. If by
chance I did hear, I could no longer see all that music
is able to unveil. Even my walks were stricken with
sterility. Things which formerly had been enough to

make me happy for the entire day—a touch of sunlight yellowing the grass, the perfume that the leaves discharged with the last drops of rain, such things had lost, as I had too, their sweetness and their gaiety. The woods, the sky, the waters, seemed to turn away from me, and when, alone with them face to face, I would anxiously question them, they no longer murmured their vague replies which had formerly enraptured me. The heavenly hosts, whose presence the voices of waters, leaves, and sky proclaim, deign only to visit those whose hearts, through living within themselves, are purified.

It was then, in searching for an inverse remedy, and because I had not the courage to will the true remedy which was so near and, alas, so far from me—deep within myself—that I allowed myself to be drawn again toward those sinful pleasures, hoping thus to rekindle the flame which society had extinguished. It was in vain. Dominated by the pleasure of pleasing, I put off from day to day the final decision, the choice, the truly free act, the option of solitude. I did not renounce one of these two vices for the other. I combined them. What am I saying? Each vice being bent on destroying all the obstacles of thought and feeling which could have stopped the other, seemed also to call the other forth. I would go into society to calm myself after sinning and then, no sooner calm, would sin again. It was at this terrible moment after I had lost my innocence and before the advent of today's remorse, at the very moment of my life when I was the most worthless, that everyone esteemed me most. I had been considered an affected, silly little girl; now, on the contrary, the ashes of my imagination. suited to the taste of society, were its delight. Just when I was committing the worst crime against my mother, everyone thought me, because of my tenderly respectful manner toward her, a model daughter. After the suicide of my mind everyone admired my intelligence, was enchanted by my wit. My dried up imagination, my arid sensibility satisfied the thirst of those most avid of an intellectual life, their thirst being as artificial and lying as the source at which they thought to quench it. No one, however, ever suspected the secret crime that was my life, and to everyone I seemed an ideal young girl. How many parents told my mother at that time, if my social position had been less brilliant, if they could have dared to think of me, they would have wished no other wife for their sons. In spite of my obliterated conscience, these undeserved praises caused me desperate shame which, however, never reached the surface, and I had fallen so low that I had the indecency to jest about them with the accomplices of my crimes.

————————————— IV —————————————

"To anyone who has lost that which can never . . . never be recovered!"

—BAUDELAIRE

In the winter of my twentieth year my mother's health, which had never been robust, grew very much worse. I learned that she had heart-disease, and while not serious, it was essential that she should be spared all anxiety. One of my uncles told me that my mother was anxious to see me married. I was faced with a definite and imperious duty. I would be able to prove to my mother how much I loved her. I accepted the first offer of marriage which she transmitted to me and which I approved, thus letting necessity, in lieu of will, force me to change my way of living. Because of his remarkable intelligence, his gentleness and energy, my fiancé was just the young man to have the happiest influence over me. Furthermore, he had resolved to live with us. I would not be separated from my mother, which would have been the most cruel of sorrows.

Now I had the courage to tell my confessor all my sins. I asked him if I should make the same confession to my fiancé. He had the compassion to advise against it but made me swear never to yield to temptation again, and gave me absolution. Belated flowers, born of joy in a heart which I had thought forever sterile, bore fruit. The grace of God, the grace of youth—through whose vitality so many wounds heal themselves—had cured me.

If, as Saint Augustine has said, it is more difficult to recover chastity than to have been chaste, I knew that difficult virtue then. No one suspected that I was worth infinitely more than before, and every day my mother kissed my forehead that she had never ceased to believe pure, not knowing that it was regenerated.

More than that, I was unjustly reproached, at this time, for my absent manner, my silence and my melancholy in society. It did not annoy me: the secret that existed between myself and my appeased conscience afforded me sufficient rapture. The convalescence of my soul—which now smiled at me with a countenance like my mother's, looking at me with tender reproach through drying tears—was infinitely languorous and sweet. Yes, my soul was being born again. I did not understand myself how I could have persecuted it, made it suffer, almost killed it. And I thanked God fervently for having saved it in time.

It was the harmony between that profound, pure joy and the fresh serenity of the sky that I was drinking in on the very evening when *all was accomplished.* The absence of my fiancé who had gone to visit his sister for two days, the presence at dinner of the young man who was principally to blame for my past sins, cast not the slightest sadness over that limpid May evening. There was not a cloud in the sky which was the perfect image of my heart. Moreover, my mother, as though there existed between her and my soul—although she knew nothing of my sins—a mysterious solidarity, had almost recovered. "You must be careful of her for another two weeks," the doctor had said, "and after that there will be no possible danger of a relapse." Those words alone were to me the promise of a future of such rapturous happiness, they made me weep for joy.

My mother, that evening, wore a gown rather more

formal than usual, and for the first time since my
father's death, although that had occurred ten years
ago, had added a touch of lavender to her customary
black. She was all confusion to be thus dressed as in
her younger days, and sad and happy to have done violence to her sorrow and her mourning in order to
give me pleasure and to celebrate my joy. I offered her
a pink carnation which she at first refused, and then,
because it came from me, pinned on with a hand a
little reluctant and ashamed. Just as we were going in
to dinner, standing near the window, I drew toward
me her face now delicately smoothed of all traces of
her past sufferings, and kissed her passionately. I was
wrong when I said that I had never felt again the
sweetness of that kiss at *Les Oublis.* The kiss of this
evening was as sweet as any other. Or rather it was the
same kiss which, evoked by the attraction of a similar
moment, had glided softly out of the depth of the past
to alight between my mother's cheeks, still a little
pale, and my lips.

We drank to my coming marriage. I never drank
anything but water because of the overstimulating
effect that wine had on my nerves. My uncle insisted
that on such an occasion as this I could make an exception. I can see his jovial face as he pronounced
those stupid words. . . . My God! My God! I have con-
fessed everything so calmly until now, must I stop
here? I can no longer see! Yes . . . my uncle said that I
could, very well, on such an occasion as this, make an
exception. He looked at me laughing as he said it. I

drank quickly without glancing at my mother for fear she would stop me. She said gently: "One should never make a place for evil, no matter how small." But the champagne was so cool that I drank two more glasses. My head grew heavy, I felt a need to rest and, at the same time, to expend my nervous energy. We rose from the table; Jacques came up to me and said, looking at me steadily, "Won't you come with me; I want to show you some poems I've written."

His beautiful eyes shone softly in his healthy face as his hand slowly stroked his mustache. I understood that I was lost and I was without power to resist. Trembling all over, I said, "Yes, I should be glad to."

It was when I uttered those words, or perhaps, even before, when I drank my second glass of champagne, that I committed the really responsible act, the abominable act. After that I did no more than let myself go. We had closed and locked the two doors, and he, his breath on my cheeks, seized me in his arms, exploring my body with his hands. Then, while more and more, pleasure took possession of me, I felt at the same time, stirring in the depth of my heart, an infinite sadness and desolation; it seemed to me that I was causing my mother's soul, the soul of my guardian angel, the soul of God to weep. I have never been able to read without shuddering with horror stories of those beasts who torture animals, their own wives, their own children; I now confusedly felt that in every sensual and sinful act there is just as much ferocity on the part of the body in the throes of pleasure, and that in us so many good intentions, so many pure angels are martyred, and weep.

Soon my uncles would have finished their game of cards and would be coming back. We would be there before them, I would never yield again, it was the last time. . . . Then, above the mantelpiece, I saw myself in the mirror. None of the vague anguish of my soul was written on my face, but everything about it, from my shining eyes to my blazing cheeks, proclaimed a sensual, stupid brutal joy. I thought then of the horror of anyone who, having observed me a little while ago kissing my mother with such melancholy tenderness, should see me thus transformed into a beast. But soon in the mirror Jacques' mouth, avid under his mustache, appeared against my cheek. Shaken to the depths of my being, I leaned my head closer to his, when I saw, yes, I tell it just as it happened, listen to me since I am able to tell you, on the balcony outside the window, I saw my mother looking at me aghast. I do not know whether she cried out. I heard nothing, but she fell backwards and lay there with her head caught between two bars of the railing. . . .

It is now the last time I tell you this: I have told you before, I almost missed myself, and yet I had aimed carefully but I fired badly. However, they could not extract the bullet and heart complications set in. Only, I may stay like this another week, and during all that time I shall be unable to stop trying to grasp the beginnings . . . never stop *seeing* the end. I should rather my mother had seen me commit still other crimes, and even that one too, than that she should have seen that look of joy on my face in the mirror. No, she could not have seen it. . . . It was a coincidence . . . she had had a stroke of apoplexy a moment before seeing me . . . she did not see it. . . . That could not be! God who knew all would not have wished it.

A Dinner in Society

"But who, Fundanius, shared with you the pleasures of
that repast? I should very much like to know."

—HORACE

——————————— I ———————————

Honoré was late. He greeted his hosts, the guests
he knew, was introduced to the others, and they
went in to dinner. After a few moments, a very young
man sitting next to him asked him to tell him the
names of the other guests and something about them.
Honoré had never seen him in society before. He was
very handsome. The hostess kept throwing ardent
glances his way which told plainly enough why he had
been invited and that he would soon become a member of her circle. He was someone with a future, Honoré felt, but without envy and with good-natured
courtesy he set about complying with his request. He
looked around the table. Opposite him the two guests
sitting side by side pointedly ignored each other. With
blundering good intention, they had been invited together and seated next to each other because they
were both engaged in literary pursuits. But besides

this foremost reason for hating each other, they had another more personal one. The elder, being related to M. Paul Desjardins and to M. de Vogüé (doubly hypnotized), affected a contemptuous silence toward the younger one, disciple and favorite of M. Maurice Barrès, who in his turn assumed an ironic expression intended for the other. Indeed, the ill-will of each exaggerated quite involuntarily the importance of the other, as though the chief of scoundrels were confronted with the king of imbeciles. Farther down the table a superb Spanish woman was eating ferociously. She had, without hesitating, like a sensible person, sacrificed another engagement this evening in order to advance her social career by dining in a fashionable house. And her calculations had had every chance of being successful. The snobbery of Madame Fremer was for her friends, and that of her friends for her, a sort of mutual guarantee against sinking into the bourgeois class. But chance would have it on this particular evening that Madame Fremer was getting rid of a stock of people she hadn't been able to dispose of before, but whom, for one reason or another, she felt obliged to entertain, and whom she had assembled tonight pell-mell. The whole lot, it is true, was topped by a duchess, but one whom the Spanish woman already knew and from whom she could expect no further advantage. She was also exchanging exasperated glances with her husband, whose guttural tones could be heard in any gathering saying successively, with a five-minute interval between each request well filled with other occupations: "Would you present me to the *Duc?*"—"*Monsieur le Duc,* would you present me to the *Duchesse?*"—"*Madame la Duchesse,* may I present my wife?" Annoyed at losing his time this evening, he had nevertheless resigned himself to the inevitable and entered into conversation with his neighbor, the partner of his host whom Fremer had been begging his wife to invite for over a year. She had finally yielded, tucking him in between the husband of the Spanish woman and a humanist. A voracious reader, the humanist was also a voracious eater. He abounded in quotations and eructations which disgusted his table companion on the other side, a noble commoner, Madame Lenoir. Without losing any time, Madame Lenoir had turned the conversation to the victories of the Prince de Buivres in Dahomey, saying in melting tones: "Dear boy, I am so glad he is such an honor to the family!" She was, it is true, a cousin of the Buivres, and they, all younger than she, treated her with all the deference due her age, her devotion to the royal family, her immense fortune and the unfailing sterility of her three marriages. Whatever family feeling she possessed she had settled on the Buivres. She felt personally dishonored by the Buivres whose misdeeds had forced his family to have a guardian appointed for him by the court, and around her right-thinking brow and Orleanist bandeaux she wore, of course, the laurels of the Buivres who was a general. An intruder in this family, hitherto so exclusive, she had become its head and, as it were, the dowager of the family. She really felt herself exiled in modern society, was always talking wistfully of "the ancient noblemen of the old days." Her snobbery was all imagination, and was, moreover, all the imagination she had. Names rich in history and glory having a strange power over her sensibilities, she found the same disinterested delight in dining with princes as in reading the memoirs of the ancient regime. Her bonnets with their grapes were as invariable as her principles. Her eyes shone with imbecility. Her smiling face was noble, her gesticulations excessive and insignificant. Trusting in God, she displayed the same flurry of optimistic excitement on the eve of a garden party or a revolution, apparently conjuring radicalism or bad weather with the same gestures. Her neighbor, the humanist, talked to her with tiresome elegance and with a terrible gift for volubility. He quoted Horace to excuse in other people's eyes, and to poetize for himself, his gluttony and drunkenness. Invisible roses, antique yet fresh, circled Madame Lenoir's narrow forehead. But with an equable courtesy (requiring no effort on her part since it represented for her the exercise of her power and respect, so rare today, for ancient traditions) every five minutes she would turn to speak to M. Fremer's partner. The latter certainly had no reason to complain. From the other end of the table Madame Fremer accorded him the most flattering attention. She wanted him to remember this dinner for many years, and, determined not to resuscitate this kill-joy for a long time to come,

she set about killing him with kindness. As for M.
Fremer, working all day at his bank and in the evening dragged by his wife into society or kept at home
when they themselves entertained, always ready to
take a person's head off, always muzzled, he had
finally acquired for all circumstances, even the most
benign, an expression which was a mixture of mute
irritation, sulky resignation, controlled exasperation
and profound and brutish insensibility. Yet this evening his wife made the financier's countenance beam
with satisfaction every time her glances and his partner's met. And although traditionally he could not
endure the man, he felt a certain fugitive but sincere
affection for him, not because he had been able to
dazzle him with his wealth, but because of that same
obscure fraternity which we feel in foreign lands at
the sight of a compatriot, no matter how unbearable.
M. Fremer, so violently wrenched from his habits
every evening, so unjustly deprived of his well-earned
repose, so cruelly uprooted, felt a bond, detested ordinarily but strong, that at last linked him to someone, drew him out, extricated him from his fierce and
desperate isolation. Opposite him, Madame Fremer
could see her blond beauty reflected in the eyes of all
the guests. The double reputation surrounding her
was a deceptive prism through which everyone tried
to make out her true character. Ambitious, given to
intrigue, almost an adventuress, according to the fi-
nancial circles she had deserted for a more brilliant
destiny, she appeared on the contrary, in the eyes of

the Faubourg and the royal family who had been se-
duced by her superior intelligence, an angel of sweetness and virtue. And, as a matter of fact, she never
forgot her more humble former friends, remembered
them particularly when they were sick or in mourning, touching circumstances, and which, moreover,
since at such times one does not go into society, made
it impossible for them to complain of not being invited. In this way she satisfied her charitable urges
and was able to shed sincere tears in the presence of
relatives and priests at the bedside of the dying, little
by little killing the remorse that her too frivolous life
inspired in her scrupulous heart.

But the most agreeable guest was the young Duchess de D . . ., whose vivacious and clear mind, that
was never perplexed or troubled, contrasted strangely
with the incurable melancholy of her beautiful eyes,
the pessimism of her lips, the infinite and noble lassi-
tude of her hands. This consummate lover of life in
all its forms—charity, literature, the theatre, action,
friendship—bit her beautiful red lips, like despised
flowers, without withering them, while they curved
ever so faintly in a smile. Her eyes seemed to betray
a spirit forever shipwrecked on the forlorn waters of
regret. How often in the street, at the theatre, thoughtful strangers had kindled their dream at those variable stars! The duchess, her thoughts at the moment
busy with the recollection of some farce she had seen,
or combining a new costume, continued nevertheless,
sadly twisting her resigned and pensive fingers, and

casting about her those deep disconsolate glances that
drowned the impressionable guests in the torrent of
their melancholy. Her exquisite conversation care-
lessly assumed the faded and charming elegances of an
outmoded skepticism. There had just been a discussion, and this person, so positive in life and who held
that there could only be one way to dress, kept repeating: "But why can't one say everything, think
everything? I may be right, you may also be right.
How terrible, how narrow to permit only one opinion." Her mind, unlike her body, was not dressed in
the latest fashion. and she would readily make fun of
the symbolists and fanatics. Her mind indeed was like
those charming women who are beautiful and vivacious enough to be attractive even dressed in dowdy
clothes. Perhaps another form of deliberate coquetry.
Certain too crude ideas would have annihilated her
mind just as certain colors were a calamity to her com-
plexion.

Honoré had given his attractive neighbor a quick
sketch of the different figures, but so good-naturedly
that, in spite of their profound differences, they all
appeared alike, the brilliant Madame de Torreno, the
witty Duchess de D . . ., the beautiful Madame Lenoir. And he had neglected the one trait they had in
common, or rather the same collective folly, the same
prevalent epidemic with which they were all afflicted:
snobbishness. And even snobbishness, according to
the nature of each, took very different forms, and it
was a far cry from the imaginative and poetic snob-

bishness of Madame Lenoir to the all-conquering
snobbishness of Madame de Torreno who was as avid
as a public official bent on getting to the top. And yet
the terrible woman was capable of being rehuman-
ized. The man sitting next to her had just finished
telling her how he had admired her little daughter in
the Parc Monceau. Immediately she broke her indignant silence. For this obscure accountant, she felt a
grateful and pure sympathy which she would perhaps have been incapable of feeling for a prince. And
they were chatting together now like old friends.

Madame Fremer presided over the conversation
with a visible satisfaction due to her consciousness of
the high mission she was accomplishing. Accustomed
to presenting noted writers to duchesses, she seemed
in her own eyes a sort of all powerful Foreign Min-
ister exercising, even over the protocol, her sovereign
judgment, just as a spectator at the theatre, as he di-
gests his dinner, looks down upon, since he judges
them, actors, audience, author, the rules of dramatic
art, genius. As a matter of fact, the conversation was
going along smoothly enough. The moment of the
dinner had been reached when the gentlemen begin
to touch knees under the table with the lady next to
them, or to inquire about her literary preferences,
depending on education and temperament, depending above all on the lady. Thus, for a second a hitch
seemed inevitable. Honoré's handsome neighbor,
with the imprudence of youth, having tried to insinu-
ate that there was perhaps in the work of Heredia

more thought than was generally supposed, the guests whose mental habits he had upset assumed a surly air. But Madame Fremer quickly exclaiming: "Oh, on the contrary, they are simply admirable cameos, gorgeous enamels, faultless specimens of the goldsmith's art," animation and satisfaction reappeared on every face. A discussion on anarchists was more serious. But Madame Fremer, as though bowing resignedly to the fatality of a natural law, said slowly: "What good would it do? Rich and poor we have always with us." And all these people, the poorest among them having an income of at least a hundred thousand pounds, impressed by the truth of her remark and relieved of their scruples, emptied with beaming cheerfulness their last glass of champagne.

------------------------ II ------------------------

After Dinner

HONORE, feeling his head a little giddy from the mixture of wines, took his departure without saying goodbye, found his coat downstairs, and started along the Champs Elysées on foot. He was overflowing with joy. The barriers of the impossible that usually keep our desires and our dreams from entering the field of reality had been broken down, and his thoughts, excited by their own motion, circulated joyously through the unattainable.

The mysterious avenues that stretch between human beings, at whose end a sun of unsuspected joy and desolation sets every evening, beckoned him. All the people he thought of became at once irresistibly sympathetic, and one after the other he took the streets where he might hope to meet them, and if his anticipations had been realized he would have greeted the unknown or indifferent person without fear and with an agreeable thrill. The stage-set too close to him having fallen, life stretched far away before him in all the charm of its novelty and its mystery in friendly landscapes that called to him. And regret that it was only the mirage or reality of a single evening filled him with despair. He would do nothing henceforth but dine and also drink, in order to see all these beautiful things again. He only suffered from his inability immediately to reach all the scenes scattered here and there in the infinitude of the distant perspective. But at that moment he became conscious of the sound of his own voice a trifle amplified, exaggerated, which for the last quarter of an hour had been repeating: "Life is sad, how idiotic!" (This last word was emphasized by an abrupt gesture of his right arm and he noticed the brusque movement of his cane.) He said sadly to himself that these mechanically uttered words were indeed a banal translation of such visions which were, perhaps, inexpressible.

"Alas! It is probably only the intensity of my pleasure and my regret that has been multiplied a hundredfold, while the intellectual narrator remains the same. My happiness is nervous, personal, untranslatable for others, and if at this moment I were to write, my style would have the same merits and the same faults and alas! the same mediocrity as usual!" But the sensation of physical well-being kept the thought from bothering him, served indeed as a supreme consolation by completely effacing it from his memory. He had arrived on the boulevards. People passed by him and he offered them his sympathy, sure that it was reciprocated. He felt himself to be the glorious center of their attention; he opened his overcoat to let them admire his gleaming white shirt front, so very becoming to him, the dark red carnation in his buttonhole. Thus he offered himself to the admiration of the passers-by and to their affection which he so voluptuously shared.

Fragments
from
Italian Comedy

> ". . . as crabs, goats, scorpions, the balance and the water-pot lose their meanness when hung as signs in the zodiac, so I can see my own vices without heat in . . . distant persons. . . ."
>
> —EMERSON

———————— I ————————

Fabrice's Mistresses

FABRICE'S mistress was intelligent and beautiful; it made him wretched. "If only she wasn't so sure of herself!" he would groan. "Her beauty is spoiled for me by her intelligence. Would I fall in love with the Joconda every time I look at her if I had to hear a critical dissertation, no matter how exquisite, at the same time?" He left her, and took another mistress who was beautiful and witless. But she would constantly prevent his enjoying her charm because of her incredible lack of tact. Then she began to aspire to intelligence, read a great deal, became a pedant and was as intellectual as the first, with less ease and with absurd ineptitudes. He begged her to be silent; but even when she was not talking her beauty painfully reflected her stupidity. Finally he made the acquaintance of a woman whose intelligence was betrayed only by a subtler grace, who was satisfied just to live, and who never dissipated by categorical observations the charming mystery of her nature. She was gentle after the fashion of agile and graceful animals, with enigmatic eyes, and was as disturbing as, in the morning, the memory of vague and poignant dreams. But she did not bother doing for him what the other two had done: she did not love him.

II

The Friends of Countess Myrto

Myrto, witty, pretty and kind, but something of a social climber, prefers to all her other friends, Parthénis who is a duchess and smarter than herself; yet she enjoys the companionship of Lalagé whose social standing is exactly equal to her own, and she is also by no means indifferent to the attractions of Cléanthis who is obscure and has no pretensions to brilliant rank. But the friend Myrto cannot endure is Doris. Doris' worldly situation is a little below that of Myrto, and she seeks out Myrto, as Myrto does Parthénis, because she is more fashionable.

If we mention these preferences and this antipathy

of Myrto, it is to point out that the Duchess Parthénis not only procures Myrto certain advantages but is free to love her for herself alone; that Lalagé also loves her for herself alone and is, in any case, a colleague belonging to the same rank—they need each other; that cherishing Cléanthis, Myrto is proud to feel that she is, after all, capable of disinterestedness, of having a sincere preference, of sympathizing, of loving, and smart enough herself to risk having a friend who is not; that, on the contrary, Doris appeals only to her snobbish ambitions without satisfying them, and like one of those little dogs eyeing a big dog guarding his bones, seeks Myrto to profit by her duchesses and possibly to pilfer one; and that finally dissatisfied by the unhappy contrast between her rank and the one to which she aspires, Myrto sees in Doris the image of her own vice. In Doris' marks of consideration for herself, Myrto does not enjoy recognizing her own friendship for Parthénis. Even Cléanthis makes her think of her ambitious dreams and Parthénis helps her realize them; Doris reminds her only of her pettiness. And being too resentful to relish playing the amusing role of patroness, she feels toward Doris the same resentment that Parthénis would feel toward her if Parthénis were not above snobbishness. She hates Doris.

─────────────── III ───────────────

Heldémone, Adelgise, Ercole

HAVING witnessed a rather indecorous scene, Ercole would not think of speaking of it to the Duchess Adelgise, but has no such scruples in regard to the courtesan, Heldémone.

"Ercole," protests Adelgise, "you don't think I should hear such a story, do you? Ah! I am very sure you are not like that with the courtesan, Heldémone. You respect me; you do not love me."

"Ercole," protests Heldémone, "can't you have the decency not to tell me such a story? I ask you frankly: are you like that with the Duchess Adelgise? You don't respect me; you can not love me."

─────────────── IV ───────────────

The Fickle Man

FABRICE who wants to, who believes he will love Beatrice forever, remembers how he also wanted to, how he also thought he would love forever, when for six months he was in love with Hyppolyta, Barbara or Clélie. Then he tries to discover in the real qualities of Beatrice a reason to believe that after his passion has died he will continue to see her, for the thought that one day he could live without seeing her is incompatible with a sentiment that enjoys the illusion of its eternity. Besides, being a circumspect egoist, he would not care to devote himself entirely—all his thoughts, his actions, his designs of the moment and his plans for the future—to a companion of a moment. Beatrice is very clever, has excellent judgment: "What a pleasure, when I am no longer in love with her, talking to her about people, about herself, about my defunct love for her . . ." (which thus converted into a more durable friendship will live again, he hopes). But when his passion for Beatrice is over he remains two years without going to see her, without having any desire to see her. One day when he is forced to call on her he fumes and stays ten minutes. Because day and night he dreams of Giulia who is singularly devoid of intelligence but whose pale gold hair smells like fragrant grass, and whose eyes are as innocent as two flowers.

V

LIFE is extraordinarily suave and sweet with certain natural, witty, affectionate people who have unusual distinction and are capable of every vice, but who make a display of none in public and about whom no one can affirm that they have a single one. There is something supple and secret about them. Besides, their perversity gives spice to their most innocent occupations, such as taking a walk in the garden at night.

——————————— VI ———————————

Lost Wax

I.

I SAW you just now for the first time, Cydalise, and I
admired first of all your blond hair that looked like a
little golden helmet on your childlike head, melancholy and pure. A rather pale red velvet gown still
further softened that singular little face in which the
lowered eyelids seemed to have imprisoned mystery
forever. But you raised your eyes; they lighted on
mine, Cydalise, and I saw in those eyes all the fresh
purity of mornings and of running water on the first
days of spring. They were like eyes that had never
looked at anything which other human eyes habitually reflect, eyes still innocent of all earthly experience. But looking at you more closely, above all I
seemed to feel something tender and hurt in you, like
someone to whom what she would have wanted had
been refused her by the fairies even before her birth.
Even stuffs on you took on a painful grace, seemed
especially sad round your arms—arms just sufficiently
discouraged to remain simple and charming. Then I
imagined that you were a princess come from very far
away down through the ages, who would now, with
languorous resignation, be forever bored, wearing
garments of a rare and ancient harmony which in our
eyes would soon take on a sweet and intoxicating fa-
miliarity. I should have liked to make you tell me

your dreams, your pains. I should have liked to see you with an ancient goblet in your hand, or rather one of those beakers with so proud and sad a form, that, empty now in our museums, hold out their drained bowls with a useless grace, but that were in other times, like you, the fresh delight of Venetian feasts, and whose last violets and roses seem still to float in the limpid current of their frothing and cloudy glass.

II.

"How can you prefer Hyppolyta to the other five women I have just named, who are incontestibly the greatest beauties of Verona? In the first place her nose is too long and beak-like."

"You should add that she has too delicate a skin and the upper lip too thin, drawing up her mouth too much when she laughs, making too sharp an angle. Yet her laugh affects me strangely, and the purest profiles leave me cold compared to the line of her nose that for you is too beak-like, for me so moving, and that reminds me of a bird. Her head too is a little like a bird, so long from the forehead to the blond nape of her neck, and even more like a bird her piercing and gentle eyes. Often at the theatre she will lean on the railing of her box; her white-gloved arm rises straight to her chin resting on the finger joints. Her perfect body swells her habitual white gauzes that are like folded wings. She makes one think of a bird dreaming on one elegant and slender leg. It is also charming to watch her feather fan fluttering and beating its white wing. I can never meet her sons or nephews, who have, all of them, the same beak-like nose, the thin lips, the piercing eyes and too delicate skins, without being moved as I recognize her race, the issue, I am sure, of a goddess and a bird. Through the metamorphosis which today shackles some winged desire in this woman's form, I recognize the little royal head of the peacock, but I look in vain behind her for the blue of the sea, the green of the sea on the feathery foam of her mythological plumage. She adds the idea of the fabulous to the thrill of beauty."

VII

Snobs

I.

A WOMAN will not hide the fact that she loves balls, horse-racing or even gambling. She says so frankly, she even boasts of it. But don't try to make her admit that she cares for Society. She will protest, will get really angry. It is the only weakness that she carefully conceals, probably because it is the only one that hurts her vanity. She has no objection to depending on cards, but not on dukes. Committing a folly does not make her feel inferior to any one; but snobbishness implies that there are people to whom she is inferior, or might be if she let herself relax. And you will often see a woman, while proclaiming the stupidity of Society, expending on its behalf an amount of shrewdness, wit and intelligence that, if she wished, would enable her to write a charming story or ingeniously vary her lover's pleasures and pains.

II.

Clever women are so afraid of being accused of loving Society that they never mention it. In the press of conversation they will make use of some circumlocution to avoid naming this compromising lover. If necessary, they seize upon the word Elegance, which turns away suspicion and at least seems to point to art rather than to vanity as the guiding factor in the ordering of their lives. Only women who have not yet been accepted by Society or those who have lost their place in it, call it by name, its ardent and unsatisfied or forsaken mistresses. Thus certain young women just launching out or old women who have fallen by the way like to talk about the people who are accepted by Society, or even better, those who are not. As a matter of fact, although talking about unsuccessful social climbers is more amusing, talking about people in Society is more nourishing and furnishes famished imaginations with a more substantial aliment. I have known women who at the mere thought of the marriages of duchesses feel thrills of pleasure rather than of envy. There are women in the provinces, it would seem, little shopkeepers whose brains are tiny cages imprisoning longings for Society as fierce as wild animals. The postman brings them the

Gaulois. The society page is gobbled up in a flash. The ravenous provincial ladies are satisfied. And for the next hour their eyes, whose pupils are inordinately dilated by veneration and delight, will shine with an expression of perfect serenity.

III.

If you were not in Society and were told that Elianthe, young, beautiful, rich, beloved by friends and lovers as she is, breaks with them, all at once, and ceaselessly courts the favor and stomachs the rebuffs of men, often ugly, old and stupid, whom she scarcely knows, works like a criminal condemned to hard labor to please them, is mad about them, becomes virtuous to please them, makes herself their friend by dint of persistence, and if they are poor, supports them, sensual, becomes their mistress, you would think: what crime must Elianthe then have committed, and who are the redoubtable magistrates whom she must placate at any price, to whom she sacrifices her friendships, her loves, her freedom of thought, the dignity of her life, her fortune, her time, and her most secret feminine aversions? Yet Elianthe has committed no crime. The judges she persists in corrupting have never given her a thought and would have let her life, happy and pure, flow tranquilly on. But there is a terrible malediction upon her: she is a snob.

IV.

Your soul, to talk like Tolstoy, is a dark forest. But the trees are of a particular species, they are genealogical trees. It is said that you are vain? But for you the universe is not empty, it is full of coats of arms. It is quite a brilliant and symbolic conception of life. Have you not your chimeras too that have the form and color of the ones painted on armorial bearings? Are you not well-informed? You have learned your *Bouillet** from *Tout-Paris,* the *Gotha,* and *High-Life.* Reading about the battles won by the illustrious ancestors, you have recognized the names of their descendants whom you entertain at dinner, and by means of this mnemotechnics carry in your head the entire history of France. This gives a certain grandeur to your ambitious dreams to which you have sacrificed your liberty, your hours of pleasure or of meditation, your duties, your friendships, even love. For in your imagination your new friends are always accompanied by their ancestral portraits. The genealogical trees you cultivate with so much care, whose fruits you gather every year with so much joy, have roots deep in the most ancient soil of France. Your dream unites the present and the past. For you, the most insignificant contemporary figure is animated by the soul of the crusades, and if you turn the pages of your engagement book so feverishly, is it not because with each name you feel awakening, quivering and almost singing, like a corpse risen from its slab, our fabulous old France!

* Marie-Nicolas Bouillet (1798-1861): Lexicographer celebrated for his two great dictionaries: *Dictionary of Our Contemporaries* and *Dictionary of History and Geography.*

VIII

Oranthe

So YOU didn't go to bed last night? You haven't washed this morning?

But why proclaim it from the house tops, Oranthe?

Brilliantly gifted as you are, isn't that enough to distinguish you from common mortals? Must you insist upon acting such a pitiful role besides?

You are hounded by creditors, your infidelities drive your wife to despair. To put on evening dress would seem to you tantamount to donning a livery, and no one could persuade you to go into society other than disheveled. Seated at dinner you keep your gloves on to prove that you are not eating, and if ever you have a fever at night you call for your victoria and go for a drive in the Bois de Boulogne.

You can read Lamartine only on a snowy night and listen to Wagner only when you smell the odor of burning cinnamon.

Yet you are a perfectly decent sort, rich enough to pay your debts if you did not think them a prerequisite of genius, tender-hearted enough to suffer from causing your wife the pain which you think it would be too bourgeois to spare her, you do not despise society, you know how to make yourself very agreeable, and your wit, without your long hair, would be enough to make people notice you. You have a good appetite, and although you eat before going to dine out, you rage inwardly at not being able to eat again. The only illnesses from which you ever suffer are those acquired on your nocturnal drives which you impose on yourself for the sake of originality. You have enough imagination to make snow fall or to smell burning cinnamon without the help of winter or an incense burner, cultured enough and musician enough to enjoy Lamartine in spirit and in truth. The trouble with you is that to the soul of an artist you have added all the prejudices of a bourgeois, only showing the reverse side and without deceiving us.

IX

Protest Against Frankness

IT IS WISE to be equally wary of Percy, Laurence and Augustin. Laurence recites poetry, Percy lectures, Augustin tells you the truth. Frankness, that is the latter's distinction and his profession; he is the true friend.

Augustin comes into a drawing room, and verily I say unto you, be on your guard, for verily he is your friend! Remember that like Percy and Laurence he never arrives with impunity, and that he will not bother to wait to be asked to tell you a few truths about yourself, any more than Laurence waits for your consent to start monologuing, or Percy to talk about Verlaine. He loses no time, permits no interruption, because he is frank, in the same way that

Laurence is a lecturer, not in your interest but for his own pleasure. Naturally your displeasure increases his pleasure, just as your attention increases that of Laurence, but he could, if necessary, get along very well without it.

So here you have three impudent scoundrels who should be refused all encouragement, enjoyment or alimentation of their vice. And yet, on the contrary, they have a special audience that applauds them. This audience, led astray by the conventional psychology of the theatre and by the absurd maxim: "Who loves, chastises," refuses to see that flattery is often only the overflowing of tenderness, and frankness the drooling of ill-humor. If Augustin practices his meanness on a friend, his audience of one mentally compares Roman ruggedness with Byzantine hypocrisy and proudly exclaims, his eyes alight with the joy of feeling himself better, tougher, less touchy than other men: "Augustin is certainly not one to mince matters . . . you have to respect him. What a true friend!"

X

A FASHIONABLE milieu is one in which everybody's opinion is made up of the opinion of all the others. Has everybody a different opinion? Then it is a literary milieu.

A libertine's need of virginity is another form of the eternal homage love pays to innocence.

Leaving the A's, you go to see the B's and the stupidity, the maliciousness, the wretched situation of the A's are laid bare. Filled with admiration for the insight of the B's, you blush to think that you had before felt a certain consideration for the A's. But when you go to see the latter again, they tear the B's to shreds, and in just about the same way. To go from one to the other is like visiting enemy camps. Only, as they never hear each other's fire, each side thinks it alone is armed. When one sees that the arms are pretty equally divided and that the forces, or rather their weakness, are about the same, one ceases to admire the one doing the shooting and to despise the one aimed at. That is the beginning of wisdom. Real wisdom would consist in breaking with both of them.

XI

Scenario

HONORE is sitting in his room. He gets up and looks at himself in the glass:

HIS TIE. Do you know how many times, with that languorous and dreamy air, you have already fixed my expressive and rather untidy knot! You must be in love, my friend. But why are you sad?

HIS PEN. Yes, why are you sad? For over a week you have been driving me relentlessly, and yet how my life has changed! I, who thought myself dedicated to the most glorious tasks, am to go on writing nothing but love letters, judging by the stock of note paper you have just received. But these love letters will be sad, as I can tell from the nervous despair with which you seize me and suddenly lay me down again. You are in love, my friend, but why are you sad?

ROSES, ORCHIDS, HORTENSIAS, MAIDEN-HAIR FERNS, COLUMBINES all over the room. You have always loved us, but never before have you called on so many of us at one time to charm you by our proud and languid poses, our eloquent gestures and the touching timbre of our perfume. For you, it is true, we represent all the fresh graces of the beloved. You are in love, but why are you sad?

THE BOOKS. We have always been your prudent counselors, always questioned, never listened to. But although we have never influenced your actions we have made you understand, so that when you rushed to your defeat you at least did not struggle in the dark and as in a nightmare: don't thrust us aside like old masters no longer wanted. You have held us in your childish hands. Your eyes, still innocent, would look at us in wonder. If you do not love us for ourselves, love us for all the memories of yourself we bring back to you, for all that you have been, for all that you might have been; and is not might have been, while one is dreaming of it, in a way, really to have been?

Come listen to our familiar and chiding voices; we will not tell you why you are in love, but we will tell you why you are sad, and if our child is in despair and weeps, we will tell him stories, we will soothe him as in the old days when his mother lent her sweet authority to our words before the fire that blazed with all its sparks and with all your hopes and dreams.

HONORE. I am in love with her and I believe I shall be loved. But my heart tells me that I who have always been so fickle will be in love with her forever, and my good fairy knows very well that I shall be loved only for a month. That is why, before entering the paradise of these brief joys, I stop on the threshold to dry my tears.

HIS GOOD FAIRY. Dear friend, I descend in pity from the skies, but your happiness depends upon yourself. Now, if for a month you will risk spoiling, by a little ruse, the joys you have been dreaming from this love, if you will treat your beloved with disdain, practice a little coquetry and affect indifference, fail to keep the appointments you make with her, and when she offers you her breasts like a bunch of roses, turn your lips away, you will build your love for eternity, faithful and shared, on the incorruptible foundation of your patience.

HONORE, leaping with joy. My good fairy, I adore you and I will obey you.

THE LITTLE DRESDEN CLOCK. Your friend is late; my hand has gone past the minute you've been dreaming of so long, at which the beloved should have arrived. I am afraid I'll have to go on for some time still marking your melancholy and voluptuous waiting with my monotonous tick-tock; although I can tell the time, I understand nothing of life. Sad hours and joyous minutes are indistinguishable in me, like bees in a hive . . .

The bell rings; a servant opens the door.

THE GOOD FAIRY. Obey me now—remember that the eternity of your love depends on it.

The clock ticks feverishly, the roses' scent is troubled, and the uneasy orchids bend anxiously toward Honoré, one of them with a nasty look. Unable to move, his pen gazes at him sadly. The books never cease their stern murmurings. All of them say to him: "Obey the fairy and remember that the eternity of your love depends on it."

HONORE, without hesitating. How can you doubt me?

The beloved enters; the roses, the orchids, the Dresden Clock and Honoré panting, all vibrate as though in tune with her.

Honoré rushes up to her, tries to kiss her lips, crying: "I love you! . . ."

EPILOGUE. It was as though he had blown out the flame of his beloved's desire. Pretending to be shocked by the unseemliness of this proceeding, she fled. And now, whenever Honoré sees her, it is only to be tortured by the indifference and the severity of her glance.

———————————— XII ————————————

The Fan

MADAME, I have painted this fan for you.

May it, in your retreat, according to your desire, call back the vain and charming forms that once peopled your drawing-room, then so full of gracious life, and now forever closed.

The chandeliers, their branches bearing great pale flowers, throw their rays over the works of art of every age and every country. As my brush followed their curious glances over all your various knickknacks, I thought of the spirit of our age. It has, like your chandeliers, contemplated samples of the thought or of the life of all ages throughout the world. It has immeasurably expanded the circle of its excursions. Out of amusement, out of boredom it has varied them as one varies one's walks, and now having given up all hope of finding not only the goal but even the right road, feeling its force and its courage failing, and not wanting to see anything any longer, it lies down with its face against the earth like a brute beast. Yet I have painted the rays of your chandeliers with tenderness; they have caressed with amorous melancholy so many things, so many people, and are now extinguished forever! In spite of the diminutive proportions of the frame, perhaps you will recognize the persons in the foreground and notice that the impartial painter, with your own unbiased sympathy, has given the same value to great noblemen, beautiful women and men of talent. Daring conciliation in the eyes of the world, insufficient and unjust, on the contrary, according to reason, but one which made of your society a less divided and more harmonious little universe than the other, yet a very lively one, and one that we shall never see again. I should not like to have my fan seen by some indifferent individual who has never frequented drawing-rooms like yours and who would be astonished to see "polite manners" able to bring together dukes without arrogance and novelists without conceit. Nor would he understand, this stranger, the vices of this surprising mixture that facilitates by the very closeness of the contact only one reciprocation—that of ridicule. Probably he will find a pessimistic realism in the spectacle he is offered by the loveseat to the right, where a great writer with every appearance of a snob listens to a great nobleman apparently holding forth on the subject of the poem he holds in his hands, and whose expression, if I have been able to make it idiotic enough, shows plainly that he doesn't understand a word of it.

Near the mantelpiece you will recognize C. . . .

He uncorks a scent bottle and explains to the woman next to him that it contains a special concentration of his own of all the most violent and exotic perfumes.

B . . . , miserable that he is unable to eclipse C, and thinking that the surest way of being ahead of the fashion is to be notoriously old-fashioned, sniffs a penny bunch of violets and looks scornfully at C. . . .

And you yourself, did you not also indulge in those artificial returns-to-nature? I should have liked, if such microscopic details could have been seen, to show in an obscure corner of your musical library of that period, your Wagner operas, your symphonies of

Franck and d'Indy laid aside, and on your piano the open scores of Haydn, of Handel or of Palestrina.

I do not hesitate to paint you on your rose-colored couch. T . . . is there, sitting beside you. He is describing how he has had his new room cleverly treated with tar to give himself the illusion of sea voyages; he expatiates on all the quintessences of his toilet table and the decorations of his room.

Your supercilious smile shows plainly enough what you think of an imagination so feeble that it is not able to call up all the visions of the universe in a perfectly bare room and that displays such a pitifully materialistic view of art and beauty.

Your most delightful friends are there. Will they ever forgive me if you show them this fan? I'm not sure. That most strangely beautiful woman, who seemed a living Whistler to our wondering eyes, would never recognize and admire herself unless painted by Bouguereau. Women are the living realizations of beauty, but they do not understand it.

They would perhaps say: We simply like a different sort of beauty. Why shouldn't it be beauty, no less than yours?

I hope at least they will permit me to say: how few women understand their own aesthetics. One of Botticelli's virgins, unless he happened to be fashionable, would consider him a bungling painter and quite devoid of talent.

I beg you to accept this fan with indulgence. If one

of the shadows, that after fluttering around my memory have settled here, once made you weep, accept it without bitterness, knowing that it is but a shadow and will never make you suffer any more.

I have been able with a clear conscience to trace these shadows on this frail paper to which your hand gives wing, since, to do any harm, they are now too frail and too unreal. . . .

No more harm perhaps than in the days when you bade them come to steal a few hours from death, and to live the vain life of phantoms in the fictitious joys of your drawing-room, under those chandeliers whose branches bore such great pale flowers.

—————————— XIII ——————————

Olivian

WHY, Olivian, are you to be seen going to the theatre every evening? Haven't your friends more wit than Pantaloon, Scaramouch or Pasquarello? and wouldn't it be more agreeable to sup with them? But you could do better still. If the theatre is the only resource for a lover of conversation whose friend is dumb and whose mistress is dull, conversation, even the most exquisite, is only the pleasure of men devoid of imagination. What an intelligent man doesn't need to be told because he learns it from talking, it is a loss of time to try to make you understand, Olivian. The voice of the imagination and of the soul is the only voice that can make the whole soul and the imagination echo happily, and if you had spent a little of the time you have killed in trying to please and had made it live instead, nourished by books or dreams, winters in front of your fire, summers in your park, you would be rich now in the memory of deeper and fuller hours. Have the courage to take up rake and hoe. And one of these days you will know the pleasure of sensing a delicious odor rising in your memory as from a garden wheelbarrow filled to the brim.

Why do you have to travel all the time? The stagecoach carries you slowly to places to which your imagination would speedily take you. You need only to close your eyes and you are at the seashore. Let those who have only bodily eyes transplant their whole households and settle in Pouzzoles or Naples. You say you must go there to finish a book? Where can you work better than in the city? Within your own four walls you can have all the grandest scenery in the world; it will be easier for you than at Pouzzoles to avoid the Princess of Bergamo's luncheons, and you will be less tempted to go for idle walks. Why, above all, do you try so hard to enjoy the present, weep because it is impossible? Having an imagination, you can never enjoy anything except through regret or expectation. In other words, you can enjoy only the past or the future.

That is why, Olivian, you are dissatisfied with your mistress, with all your wanderings, and with yourself. Perhaps you are already aware of the reason for these evils; then why do you put up with them instead of trying to cure them? Because, Olivian, you are truly unfortunate. Because, almost before you were a man, you were already a man of letters.

—————————— XIV ——————————

Actors in the Comedy of Society

JUST as in the Italian comedy Scaramouch is always the boaster, Harlequin always the dunce, just as Pasquino's conduct is nothing but intrigue, that of Pantaloon made up of avarice and credulity; so society has decreed that Guido is witty but perfidious, and would not hesitate to sacrifice his best friend for the sake of an epigram; that Girolamo under a rude armor of frankness conceals treasures of sensibility; that Castruccio, whose vices one must of course decry, is the most faithful of friends and the most attentive of sons; that Iago, in spite of the ten books to his credit, is only an amateur, while Ercole's few bad articles in the newspapers have won him the title of author; that Césare must have some connection with the police, must be an informer or a spy. Cardenio is a snob, Pippo's geniality, in spite of all his protestations of friendship, is false. As for Fortunata, it has been decided once and for all: she is kind. Her abundant curves are sufficient guarantees of the benevolence of her character: how could anyone as fat as she is be malicious?

Each one of them, moreover, so different by nature to begin with from the character that society has found for him in its general warehouse of costumes and characters and given him for all time, deviates all the more willingly from his true character since the *a priori* conception of his virtues, in opening a large credit for his opposite faults, creates to his advantage a sort of impunity. His immutable character of faithful friend in general, allows Castruccio to betray each one of his friends in particular. The friend alone suffers: "What a scoundrel he must be to be dropped by Castruccio, such a faithful friend!" Fortunata can spread oceans of scandal with impunity. Who would be mad enough to go looking for their source in those rolls of fat, whose vastness could conceal almost anything? Girolamo can make use of flattery without the slightest apprehension; it only adds an unexpected charm to his habitual frankness. He can be rude to a friend to the point of ferocity, since it is understood that it is in the friend's own interest he is being so roughly handled. Césare asks me about my health, it is only to gossip about it to the Doge. He has not asked about it: how well he knows how to hide his game! Guido comes up to me, he compliments me on looking so well. Everyone present exclaims in chorus: "No one is wittier than Guido, but he is really too malicious!" This divergence between the true character of Castruccio, of Guido, of Cardenio, of Ercole, of Pippo, of Césare, of Fortunata and the types they irrevocably incarnate in the sagacious eyes of society, is without the least danger for them, since society refuses to see it. But it is not without end. No matter what he may do, Girolamo is a beneficent brute. No matter what Fortunata may say, she is kind. The absurd, overpowering, immutable persistence of the type from which they constantly diverge without in any way disturbing its divine fixity ends by imposing itself with an ever growing force of attraction on these persons themselves, almost devoid of originality or consistency of behavior, so that they end up by being fascinated by this identity that remains immutable in the midst of their eternal variations. Girolamo, in telling his friend the "plain truth," is really grateful to him for being his butt, allowing him in "chiding him for his own good" to play an honorable, an almost brilliant role which is now almost sincere. He mingles with the violence of his diatribes an indulgent pity, very natural toward an inferior who serves to increase his reputation; he positively feels gratitude toward his friend, and the kindliness society has lent him all this time, he finally acquires. Fortunata, whose expanding flesh, without affecting her wit or altering her beauty, in extending the sphere of her own personality has made her less interested in other people's affairs. Her acrimony, which was the only thing that prevented her from discharging worthily the honorable and charming functions that the world has assigned her, she now feels being mollified. The spirit of the words "benevolence," "kindness," "joviality," which, coming and going, she keeps hearing pronounced, has gradually affected her conversation which, always laudatory now, is lent an even more flattering weight by the vastness of her proportions. She has a vague but profound feeling that she is exercising a considerable and pacific magistracy. Sometimes overflowing her own individuality, society appears to her as the plenary assembly, tempestuous, yet docile, over which she presides, and the approbation of these benevolent judges moves her as from afar. . . .

And when, on evenings given over to conversation, not worrying in the least about the contradictions in the behavior of these actors, not noticing their slow adaptation to the type imposed on them, everyone mentally files their actions neatly away in their proper drawer marked with their ideal characteristics, everyone feels with a thrill of satisfaction that the level of conversation has incontestably risen. Naturally these labors are interrupted in time, before these good people, whose heads are not much given to abstractions, fall asleep (one knows how to behave in society). And so, after having blasted this one's snobbery, that one's maliciousness and the libertinism or the insensibility of a third, the company breaks up, and everyone, convinced that he has paid generously his tribute to benevolence, modesty, and charity, goes away to indulge, without remorse and with a clear conscience, the elegant vices he particularly cultivates.

These reflections, inspired by the society of Bergamo, would lose a portion of their truth if applied to any other. When Harlequin left the Bergamo stage for the French stage, from being a dunce he became a wit. In the same way, in certain societies, Liduvina is regarded as an exceptional woman and Girolamo a clever man. It should be added that sometimes a man will appear in society for whom it has no ready-made character or at least none that is not being used at the moment by somebody else. First they give him one that doesn't suit him at all. If he is a man of real originality and there is nothing his size in stock, incapable of trying to understand him and for lack of a character to fit him, society ostracizes him; unless, of course, he can gracefully play the young juvenile who is always in demand.

Violante
or
Worldly Vanities

"Beware the company of young men and of persons of the
great world. . . . Do not seek to be seen in the company of
the great."

—*Imitation of Jesus Christ, Book I, Chapter VIII*

———————— I ————————

The Meditative Childhood of Violante

THE VISCOUNTESS OF STYRIA was generous and tender and charmed everyone by her grace. Her husband, the Viscount, had a very lively disposition and
features of an admirable regularity. But the first gren-
adier who came along was more sensitive and less
vulgar than he. In the rustic domain of Styria, far
removed from the world, they reared their daughter
Violante who, beautiful and lively like her father, as
charitable and mysteriously seductive as her mother,
seemed to unite in the most harmonious proportions
the best of both parents. But the variable aspirations
of her heart and of her mind failed to meet with a
will that would have guided, without trammeling

them, and have prevented her from becoming their charming and fragile toy. This lack of will power inspired in Violante's mother fears that might with time have borne fruit if the Viscountess with her husband had not, while out hunting one day, met with a violent end, leaving Violante an orphan at fifteen. Living almost entirely alone under the vigilant but bungling supervision of old Augustin, her tutor and the intendant of the Castle of Styria, for lack of friends Violante made charming companions of her dreams, vowing to remain faithful to them all her life. They went with her on all her walks, along the avenues of the park, across the countryside, or idled with her on the terrace which, separating the domain of Styria, looks toward the sea. By them reared, as it were above herself, initiated by them, Violante was sensitive to all visible things, sensed to a certain extent the invisible. Her joy was infinite, interrupted by moments of sadness that surpassed even her joy in sweetness.

——————— II ———————

Sensuality

"Lean not upon a reed that the wind sways, and put not thy faith in it, for all flesh is as grass and its glory passeth like the flower of the fields."

—*Imitation of Jesus Christ*

EXCEPT for Augustin and a few native children of Styria, Violante saw no one. Only a younger sister of

Violante

her mother who lived at the Castle of Julianges, situ-
ated about an hour's distance away, occasionally came
to visit Violante. One day coming to see her niece in
this way, she brought with her a young friend. He was
sixteen years of age and his name was Honoré. He did
not please Violante, but he came again. While they
strolled through the avenues of the park, he talked to
her of most unseemly things she had never before
suspected. They gave her an exquisite pleasure of
which, however, immediately she felt ashamed. Then
as the sun had set and as they had been walking for a
long time, they sat down on a bench to admire, no
doubt, the rosy sky reflected in the sea. Honoré drew
closer to Violante to keep her from feeling cold, and
with ingenious deliberation, fastened the fur around
her throat. He suggested that they might now try putting into practice the theories he had been teaching
her in the park. He spoke to her in a whisper, his lips
close to her ear, and she did not draw away. But they
heard a noise among the leaves. "It is nothing," said
Honoré tenderly. "It is my aunt," said Violante. It
was the wind. But Violante, who had risen, cooled
most opportunely by this little wind, would not sit
down again and left Honoré in spite of his entreaties.
She felt remorse, had a fit of hysterics, and for two
nights in succession could not get to sleep for a very
long time. Her confidant was her burning pillow
which she turned and turned again. Two days later
Honoré asked to see her. She had them tell him she
had gone for a walk. Honoré, feeling that this was not

true, was afraid to come again. The next summer she thought of Honoré with tenderness, with grief too, for she knew that he had gone to sea as a sailor. When the sun had disappeared, sitting on the bench where they had sat together a year ago, she tried to remember Honoré's lips held out to her, his half-closed green eyes, his vagabond glances like rays suffusing her with their warm and living light. And on sweet nights, on vast and secret nights, when the certainty that no one could see her excited her desire, she would hear the voice of Honoré whispering forbidden things in her ear. She conjured him up entire, haunting and offered like a temptation. One evening at dinner she sighed as she looked at her tutor sitting opposite her.

"I am very sad, dear Augustin," said Violante, and added, "I have no one who loves me."

"And yet," replied Augustin, "when I went to Julianges to arrange the library a week ago, I heard someone say of you: 'How beautiful she is!' "

"Who was it?" Violante asked sadly.

A faint smile lifted the corner of her lip as one lifts a curtain to let in a little of the gaiety of the day.

"It was the young man who came to see you last year, M. Honoré. . . ."

"I thought he was at sea," said Violante.

"He has come back," said Augustin.

Violante quickly left the table and went unsteadily to her room, where she wrote inviting Honoré to come to see her. Taking up her pen she had a feeling of happiness and power, hitherto unknown to her, the feeling that she was arranging her life a little according to her own whim and for her pleasure, that after all, she could give the wheels of their two destinies which seemed to have kept them mechanically apart, a little push with her finger, that he would appear on the terrace and not as in the cruel ecstasy of her unsatisfied desire, that between her unspoken tendernesses—her perpetual interior romance—and real things, there were avenues of communication along which she would hasten toward the impossible which, in creating, she would make viable. The next day she received Honoré's reply. Trembling, she went to read it on the bench where he had kissed her.

Dear Miss Violante,
    Your letter comes to me one hour before my ship sails. We made port only for one week, and it will be four years before I return again. May I hope that you will deign to remember
                    Your respectful and tender
                                            Honoré

Then, gazing at this terrace where he would never come again, where no one would come to satisfy her desire, and at this sea which was taking him away from her and giving her in exchange, in her young girl's imagination, a little of its immense charm, mysterious and sad, the charm of things that are not ours, and that reflect too many skies, too many shores, Violante burst into tears.

"My poor Augustin," she said that evening, "a great grief has come to me."

Her first feeling of the need of confiding in someone was born of her first sensual disappointment as
naturally as it is ordinarily born of love's first satis-
factions. She did not yet know love. But it was not
long before love made her suffer, which is the only
way one ever comes to know it.

—————————— III ——————————

The Pangs of Love

VIOLANTE was in love, that is to say, a young English-
man, by the name of Laurence, had for several months
occupied all her most insignificant thoughts, been the
goal of her most important actions. She had gone
hunting with him once, and could not understand
why, ever since, the desire to see him again dominated
all her thoughts, drove her to look for him along all
the surrounding roads, kept her from sleeping, destroyed her peace and happiness. Violante loved and
Violante was spurned. Laurence loved the world, and
to go where he went, Violante learned to love it too.
But Laurence had no eyes for this twenty-year-old
country girl. She fell ill from grief and jealousy, went
to the waters of . . . to forget Laurence, but her pride
was incurably wounded from having seen so many
unworthy women preferred to herself, and she decided to triumph over them by acquiring their advantages.

"I am leaving you, my good Augustin," she said. "I am going to the Austrian court."

"God help us," said Augustin. "What will the poor people here do without your charities while you are living in the midst of all those wicked people? You will no longer play with our children in the woods. Who will play the organ at the church? We shall no longer see you painting in the fields, you will no longer compose your songs for us."

"Don't worry, Augustin," said Violante; "just keep my castle beautiful and my peasants of Styria faithful. The world for me is only a means to an end. It gives one vulgar but invincible arms, and if some day I am to be loved, I shall have need of them. Curiosity also impels me and the need of living a rather more material life, and less meditative, than the one I lead here. It is both a vacation and a school I seek. As soon as I have made a name for myself in the world, and my vacation is over, I shall leave it and return to the country, to our good simple people, and to what I love best of all, my songs. At a certain moment, not too far off, I shall stop myself on the downward path and I shall come back to our Styria to live with you, dear Augustin."

"But will you then be able to?" said Augustin.

"One can do what one wants to do," said Violante.

"Perhaps you will not want the same things then," said Augustin.

"Why?" asked Violante.

"Because you will have changed," said Augustin.

─────────────── IV ───────────────

Worldly Vanities

THE PEOPLE of the great world are so mediocre that
Violante had only to condescend to mix with them to
eclipse them, almost all. The haughtiest noblemen,
the most untamed artists sought her out and courted
her. She alone had a wit, a taste, a bearing that stirred
thoughts of all other perfections. She launched plays,
perfumes, dresses. Dressmakers, writers, hairdressers
begged her patronage. The most famous milliner of
Austria asked permission to call herself Violante's exclusive modiste; one of the most illustrious princes of
Europe asked permission to call himself her lover. She
decided to refuse them both this mark of her esteem,
which would forever have conferred on them the
stamp of elegance. Among the young men who asked
to be received by Violante, Laurence made himself
conspicuous by his persistence. After having caused
her so much unhappiness, he now inspired in her, for
that very reason, a certain repugnance. And his ab-
jection kept her from him more inevitably than his
indifference had once kept him from her. "I have no
right to be shocked," she said to herself. "I did not
love him for the nobility of his soul, and knew very
well, although I would not admit it to myself, that
he was vile. It did not prevent my loving him, but
only prevented my loving nobility of soul as much. I
believed that one could be vile and at the same time

amiable. But as soon as one no longer loves, one begins to prefer people with a heart. How strange was my passion for that evil man, the product solely of my imagination for which I had not even the excuse of being carried away by my senses! Platonic love means very little!" We shall see a little later on how she came to feel that sensual love meant even less.

Augustin came to see her, wanted to take her back to Styria.

"You have conquered a veritable kingdom," he said to her. "Is that not enough for you? Why not be the old Violante again!"

"I have only just conquered it, Augustin," replied Violante. "Let me at least rule over it for a few months."

An event which Augustin had not foreseen now exempted Violante for the moment from all thought of retirement. After refusing twenty serene highnesses, as many sovereign princes and a genius, she married the Duke of Bohemia, who had any number of attractions and five million ducats. Honoré's unexpected return the day before the ceremony came very near to breaking up the marriage, but he was suffering from some disfiguring malady that rendered his familiarities odious to Violante. She wept over the vanity of those desires that had once flown so ardently toward her awakening senses, and that were already withered forever. The Duchess of Bohemia continued to exert her charms as had Violante of Styria, and the Duke's immense fortune but served to provide a worthy frame for the work of art she was. But from a work of art she became an article of luxury through that natural propensity of things here below to descend even lower when no noble effort any longer holds their center of gravity above themselves. Augustin was astonished by all the things he heard about her. "Why," he wrote, "does the duchess speak continually of things that Violante despised?"

"Because I should be less popular if I were preoccupied with things which, by their very superiority, are detestable and incomprehensible to people of society," replied Violante. "But I am bored, my good Augustin."

He came to see her, explained to her why she was bored: "You no longer exercise your taste for music, for meditation, for charity, for solitude, for the country. You think only of success; you are ruled by pleasure. But happiness is to be found only in doing what one loves, following the soul's profoundest bent."

"How can you know that, you who have never lived?" said Violante.

"I have thought, and that is to live," said Augustin. "But I hope that soon you will be overcome by disgust for this insipid life."

Violante became more and more bored, she was no longer gay. Then the world's immorality, which till now had left her indifferent, affected her all at once and hurt her cruelly, just as the seasons' inclemencies shatter bodies which through illness have grown incapable of resistance. One day as she was walking alone in a deserted avenue of the park, from a carriage she had not heard approaching, she saw a woman descend and come directly toward her. Addressing her, the woman asked if she were Violante of Bohemia, telling her that she had been a friend of her mother and had longed to see the little Violante whom she had so often dandled on her knees. She kissed her with emotion, put her arm around her waist, and began kissing her again and again in such a way that Violante, without stopping to say goodbye, took to her heels. The following evening Violante went to an entertainment given in honor of the Princess of Misena whom she did not know. In the princess she recognized the abominable woman of the day before. And a dowager whom Violante, until that moment, had respected highly, said to her, "Would you like me to introduce you to the Princess of Misena?"

"No!" said Violante.

"You mustn't be shy," said the dowager. "I am sure you would please her. She is fond of pretty young women."

From that day Violante had two mortal enemies, the dowager and the princess, who went about everywhere calling her a monster of pride and perversity. Hearing this, Violante wept for herself and for the wickedness of women. She had long ago made up her mind about that of men. Soon she began saying to her husband every evening, "Tomorrow we will go to my Styria and we will never leave it again."

But then there would be an entertainment she thought she might enjoy more than the others, a prettier gown to display. The profound needs of imagination, of solitude and of thought, and also of self-sacrifice, while making her suffer because they were not satisfied, while preventing her from finding the least shadow of satisfaction in society, were too weakened now, were no longer imperious enough to change her way of life, to force her to renounce the world and to realize her true destiny. She continued to offer the garish and desolate spectacle of an existence made for the infinite, little by little reduced almost to a void, with nothing left but the melancholy shadows of the noble destiny that might have been hers, and from which she drew away farther and farther every day. A great impulse toward true philanthropy, that like a tide would have cleansed her heart, leveled all human inequalities which block the worldly heart, was stopped by the thousand dams of selfishness, coquetry and ambition. Kindness pleased her now only as an elegant gesture. She still was generous of her money, her trouble and her time, but a whole side of herself had been relinquished, no longer belonged to her. Mornings in bed she would still read or dream, but with a distorted mind that stopped short at the outside of things and would contemplate itself not with a desire to penetrate more profoundly, but to admire itself voluptuously and coquettishly, as in a mirror. And if someone were announced she would not have the courage to send the visitor away, to continue to read and to dream. She had arrived at the point where she could no longer enjoy nature except with perverted senses, and the charm of the seasons now existed for her only to heighten the savor of mundane things, and to give them their tonality. The charm of winter became the exhilarating sensation of cold and the gaiety of the chase closed her heart to the melancholy of autumn. Sometimes by walking alone in the forest she would try to find the natural source of true joys. But under the shady leaves she continued unconsciously to display her brilliant gowns. And the pleasure of being elegant spoiled for her the joy of being alone and dreaming.

"Are we leaving tomorrow?" inquired the duke.

"Day after tomorrow," replied Violante.

Then the duke stopped asking. To Augustin, who complained, Violante wrote: "I shall return when I am a little older." "Ah!" replied Augustin, "you are deliberately giving them your youth; you will never return to your Styria." She never returned. Young, she stayed in the world to rule over the kingdom of fashion that, hardly more than a child, she had conquered. Grown old, she stayed on to defend it. All in vain. She lost it. And when she died she was still engaged in trying to re-conquer it. Augustin had counted on disgust. But he had counted without a force which, if nourished from the first by vanity, will overcome disgust, contempt, and even boredom: and that is habit.

August, 1892

The Social Ambitions and Musical Tastes
of
Bouvard and Pécuchet*

─────────────── I ───────────────

Social Ambitions

"NOW THAT WE HAVE a situation," said Bouvard, "why shouldn't we go into society?"

Pécuchet was inclined to agree with him, but still, one ought to shine in society, and for that it would be necessary to make a study of the subjects that are treated there.

Contemporary literature is of prime importance.

They subscribed to the numerous reviews in which it is disseminated, read them aloud, endeavored to write criticisms, and, bearing in mind the purpose they had in view, aimed especially at a light and airy style.

Bouvard objected, however, that the critical style, no matter how playfully handled, was not suitable for

* The opinions here lent to Flaubert's two famous characters are not, of course, those of the author.

society. And they instituted conversations between themselves on what they had read, endeavoring to imitate people in society.

Bouvard would lean his elbow on the mantelpiece, toying cautiously, so as not to soil them, with a pair of light-colored gloves brought out for the occasion, calling Pécuchet "Madame" or "Général," to complete the illusion.

But they would often get no further, one of them being invariably carried away by his enthusiasm for an author, the other trying to restrain him. And besides, they disparaged everything. Leconte de Lisle was too unemotional, Verlaine had too much sensibility. They dreamed of a middle course without ever finding it.

"Why can't Loti ever change his tune?"

"His stories are always on the same note."

"He has only one string to his lyre."

"But André Laurie is not much more satisfying, for every year he takes you to a different place, confusing geography and literature. His style alone has some value. As for Henri de Régnier, he is either crazy or a faker; there is no other alternative."

"Get around that one, old man," said Bouvard, "and you will save contemporary literature from an impossible dilemma."

"Why press them?" said Pécuchet with kingly tolerance. "There's hot blood in these young colts perhaps. Just give them their heads—the only danger is that once they start running away they may go beyond the goal; yet extravagance is itself a proof of a rich nature.

"But meanwhile all the barriers will be broken down," Pécuchet went on excitedly, filling the peaceful room with his contradictions. "And what's more, you can say all you like that these uneven lines are verse, I refuse to admit that they are anything but prose, and pure nonsense at that!"

Mallarmé has no more talent than the others, but is a brilliant talker. What a pity that such a gifted man should go mad as soon as he picks up his pen. A strange disease which seemed to them inexplicable. Maeterlinck knows how to startle, but only by using material means unworthy of the theatre; making art as thrilling as a crime—it's disgraceful! His syntax moreover is wretched.

They then proceeded to criticize him in a witty parody, using the form of a conjugation:

"I said that the woman had come in.
"Thou saidst that the woman had come in.
"You said that the woman had come in.
"Why did they say that the woman had come in?"

Pécuchet wanted to send this little piece to the *Revue des Deux Mondes,* but Bouvard thought it would be wiser to reserve it for their entrance into society and launch it in some fashionable drawing room. They would immediately be classed as they deserved. Later, they could very well send it to some review. And those who had been the first to appreciate the witticism, seeing it in print later on would be flattered to have had the first fruits.

Lemaître, in spite of all his cleverness, seemed to them inconsequential, irreverent, at times pedantic, at others bourgeois; too often he was forced to sing the palinode. And besides, his style was careless, but the difficulty of writing hurriedly in order to be ready at fixed dates that came so close together partly absolved him. As for France, he is a good writer but a bad thinker, the contrary of Bourget who is profound but with no sense of form. They felt sad at the scarcity of genuine talent.

And yet it ought not to be so difficult, Bouvard felt sure, to express one's thoughts clearly. But clarity is not enough, grace too (combined with forcefulness) is necessary, vivacity, elevation, and logic. He added irony. But in Pécuchet's opinion irony is not indispensable; more often than not it fatigues and confuses the reader without benefiting him. In short, everybody writes badly. According to Bouvard the excessive desire for originality is to blame; according to Pécuchet it is due to the decadence of our morals.

"We must have the courage to hide our conclusions in society," said Bouvard. "We would be regarded as slanderers and, frightening everyone, we would make ourselves generally unpopular. Our originality will do us enough harm as it is and we should make every effort to hide it. Better avoid talking literature in society."

But there are other things that are important in society.

"Take the question of bowing. Should one bow with the whole body, or the head only, slowly or quickly, just as one is or bringing the heels together, advancing or standing still, drawing in the small of the back or using it as a hinge? Should the hands hang straight at one's side, should one keep one's hat, wear gloves? During the salutation, should one's expression remain serious or should one smile? But how is one to resume one's gravity quickly when the salutation is over?"

Introducing people is another problem.

Whose name should one say first? Should one motion to the person one names or just nod the head in his direction, or remain motionless with an air of indifference? Should one bow in the same way to an old man and to a young man, to a locksmith and a prince, to an actor and an academician? An affirmative answer suited Pécuchet's principles of equality but it shocked Bouvard's common sense.

And how about titles?

One says *"Monsieur"* to a baron, a viscount, a count; but *"Bonjour Monsieur le Marquis"* seemed servile, and *"Bonjour Marquis,"* too cavalier. They decided to say "Prince" and *"Monsieur le Duc."* When it came to a question of highnesses, they were perplexed. Bouvard, flattered by his future connections, imagined a thousand phrases in which this appellation appeared in all its forms; he accompanied it with a blushing little smile, bowing his head slightly and giving a little skip. But Pécuchet declared that he would be sure to get mixed up or would laugh right in the prince's face. In short, to avoid embarrassment they decided not to frequent the Faubourg Saint-Germain. But the Faubourg goes everywhere nowadays, and it is only from a distance that it seems compact and isolated! . . . Besides, titles are respected even more in the society of high finance, and as for all the foreign upstarts, their titles are innumerable. But according to Pécuchet one has to be pitiless with these false nobles and make a point of not using their titles even on envelopes or when speaking to their servants. Bouvard, more of a skeptic, regarded their mania as simply more recent but just as respectable as that of the ancient nobility. Besides, according to Bouvard and Pécuchet, the nobility no longer existed since it had lost its privileges. They are all clerical, backward, never open a book, idle, and just as bent on pleasure as the bourgeoisie; to honor them they thought absurd. Frequenting the nobility was only possible for them if they reserved to themselves the right to despise them. Bouvard said that in order to know what houses they should frequent, and the correct places to go in the summer, what habits and what vices they would adopt, it would be necessary to draw up an exact plan of Parisian Society. It consisted of the Faubourg Saint-Germain, high finance, the foreign upstarts, Protestant society, the world of the arts and the theatre, the official and the learned world. The

Faubourg, in Pécuchet's opinion, under a rigid appearance, concealed all the vices of the ancient regime. Every noble has mistresses; a nun conspires with the clergy. They are brave, always in debt, ruin and abuse the money lenders, and are the inevitable champions of honor. They rule by elegance, invent extravagant fashions, are exemplary sons, gracious to the common people, arrogant to bankers. They always have a sword in their hand and a woman mounted on the saddle behind them; they dream of the restoration of the monarchy, are terribly idle, but not proud with simple people, insult cowards, make traitors fly, and by a certain air of chivalry merit our unbounded regard.

On the contrary, high finance, formidable and irascible, inspires respect but also aversion. The financier is harassed even at the gayest balls. One of his innumerable employees always comes to give him the latest news of the Stock Exchange, even at four o'clock in the morning; he hides his luckiest strokes from his wife, his worst disasters. You never quite know whether he is a tycoon or a swindler; he is both, turn and turn about without warning, and in spite of his immense fortune, he will pitilessly dispossess a poor tenant unable to pay his rent, allowing him an extension only if he wants to use him as a spy or to sleep with his daughter. Besides, he is never out of his carriage, dresses without taste, always wears eyeglasses.

They felt just as little enthusiasm for Protestant society; it is cold, stiff, gives only to its own charities, and is made up exclusively of preachers. Their temples look too much like their houses, and their houses are as dreary as their temples. They always have a preacher for dinner; the servants quote the Bible when they have some objection to make to their masters; their fear of all gaiety is sure proof that they have something to hide, and in their conversation with Catholics they betray their undying rancor over the Edict of Nantes and the Massacre of St. Batholomew.

The world of the arts is just as homogeneous but very different. Every artist is a trifler, at odds with his family, never wears an opera hat, speaks a special jargon. They spend their lives thinking up tricks to play on bailiffs who come to attach their possessions and grotesque costumes to wear to masked balls. Yet they are always producing masterpieces and, with most of them, their excessive enjoyment of women and wine is the necessary concomitant of their inspiration, if not the cause of their genius. They sleep all day, wander about all night, work nobody knows when, they throw back their heads to let their broad ties float in the wind, and never stop rolling cigarettes.

The world of the theatre can hardly be distinguished from the world of art. Family life is unknown, everybody is fantastically and inexhaustibly generous. Actors, although vain and jealous, are always ready to help their comrades, applaud their successes, adopt the children of tubercular or needy actresses, are useful in society although, having had no education, they are often religious and always superstitious. Those belonging to the subsidized theatres are in a class apart, altogether worthy of our admiration, deserving the place of honor at table before a general or a prince, and their souls are filled with all the sentiments expressed in the masterpieces they perform in our great theatres. . . . Their memories are prodigious and their manners perfect.

As for the Jews, without condemning them (one must be liberal), Bouvard and Pécuchet admitted that they detested being with them. All Jews once sold opera-glasses in Germany when they were young, have retained—and with a piety to which as impartial critics we must do justice—their religious observances, an unintelligible vocabulary, and butchers of their own race. They all have hooked noses, exceptional minds, and servile souls that think of nothing but making money; their wives on the contrary are beautiful, a trifle flabby but capable of lofty sentiments. How many Catholics would do well to imitate them! But why was their fortune always incalculable and mysterious? Besides, they formed a sort of vast secret society like the Jesuits and the Freemasons. They all had inexhaustible treasures, nobody knows where, at the service of vague enemies for some horrible and mysterious end.

II

Musical Tastes

ALREADY disgusted with bicycles and painting, Bouvard and Pécuchet now seriously took up music. While Pécuchet, the eternal friend of tradition and order, was willing to let himself be hailed as the last partisan of ribald songs and of the *Domino Noir,* revolutionary if there ever was one, Bouvard, it must be admitted, "showed himself resolutely Wagnerian." As a matter of fact he had never heard a score of that "Brawler of Berlin" (as Pécuchet, always patriotic and always misinformed, cruelly called him) for they cannot be heard in France where the *Conservatoire* is dying of routine between the stutterings of *Colonne* and the lispings of *Lamoureux,* nor in Munich that has lost the tradition, nor in Bayreuth spoiled by the snobs. They are nonsense played on the piano; they require the illusion of the stage as well as an orchestra under the stage, and in the hall, darkness. However, ready to dumbfound visitors, the prelude to *Parsifal* was perpetually open on the piano, between the photographs of César Franck's pen-holder and Botticelli's "Spring."

From the score of the *Walkyrie,* the "Spring Song" had been carefully torn out, and in the list of Wagner's operas on the first page an indignant red pencil had drawn a line through *Lohengrin* and *Tannhauser. Rienzi* alone of the early operas was allowed to remain. Disowning it was now too banal, and Bouvard sensed that the moment had come to inaugurate the contrary opinion. Gounod made him laugh, and Verdi made him scream. Who, least of all Erik Satie, would contradict him? Beethoven, however, seemed to them considerable after the manner of a Messiah, and Bouvard could, without shame, hail Bach as his own precursor. Saint-Saëns lacked depth and Massenet form, as he kept telling Pécuchet who always rejoined that Saint-Saëns, on the contrary, had only depth and Massenet only form.

"That is why the first instructs us," Pécuchet would insist, "and the second charms without elevating us."

For Bouvard, both were equally despicable. Massenet sometimes had ideas but trite ones, and besides, ideas have had their day. Saint-Saëns had a certain skill, but old-fashioned. Knowing little about Gaston Lemaire, but playing with contrasts at times, they would pit Chausson against Chaminade. Pécuchet, moreover, and even Bouvard, in spite of his aesthetic repugnances (for every Frenchman is chivalrous and always lets women go first), gallantly yielded first place to Chaminade among the composers of the day.

In Bouvard it was much more the democrat than the musician who denounced the music of Charles Levadé. For is it not running counter to progress to dwell on the poetry of Madame de Gerardin in this age of steam, universal suffrage and the bicycle? Besides, believing as he did in the theory of art for art's sake, in colorless playing and inflectionless singing,

Bouvard declared he could not bear to hear him sing, finding him too "musketeer," with swaggering manners and the too facile elegance of an antiquated sentimentality.

But the subject of their most animated debates was Reynaldo Hahn. While his intimacy with Massenet constantly provoked the unkind sarcasms of Bouvard, and pitilessly marked him as the victim of Pécuchet's passionate prejudices, he had also the gift of exasperating the latter by his admiration for Verlaine, shared, as a matter of fact, by Bouvard. Why couldn't he use texts by Jacques Normand, Sully Prudhomme, Vicomte Borelli? "God be thanked," he would patriotically add, "in the land of the troubadours there is no dearth of poets!" And, divided between the Teutonic sonority of Hahn and the meridional ending of his Christian name Reynaldo, Pécuchet preferred to condemn him because of his own hatred for Wagner rather than to absolve him in consideration of Verdi and would conclude sternly, turning toward Bouvard: "In spite of the efforts of all your fine gentlemen, our beautiful country of France is still the country of clarity, and French music will be clear, or there will be no French music." And he would strike the table with all his might to emphasize his words.

"A plague on all your eccentricities from across the North Sea, and on your fogs from beyond the Rhine; you should stop always looking over the tops of the Vosges!"—and he would add, fixing his eyes severely and significantly on Bouvard—"except for the defense

of the fatherland. I doubt if the *Walkyrie* is even liked
in Germany . . . but to French ears it will always be
the most infernal torture—and the most cacaphonic!
and, let me add, the most humiliating to our national
pride. What's more, doesn't this opera combine everything that is most atrocious in the way of dissonance
with everything that is most revolting in the way of
incest! Your music, Sir, is full of monsters, and one
would be at a loss to know what more to invent. Even
in nature—mother of simplicity—you like only the
horrible! Doesn't M. Delafosse even write songs about
bats, in which the extravagance of the composer is
sure to compromise the time-honored reputation of
the pianist? Why doesn't he choose a charming bird?
Songs about sparrows would at least be very Parisian.
The swallow has lightness and grace, and the skylark
is so eminently French that Caesar had them stuck, all
roasted, on his soldiers' helmets. But bats!!! French-
men, forever thirsting for sincerity and light, will always execrate that animal of darkness. In M. de Mon-
tesquiou's verses it is different, the whim of a great
and blasé nobleman which we may, at a pinch, con-
done—but in music! . . . I wonder when they will give
us a *Requiem of the Kangaroos?*" Bouvard was forced
to smile at this humorous sally. "Admit that I have
made you laugh," said Pécuchet (without any reprehensible fatuity, for the consciousness of one's own
merit is excusable in men of wit). "Let's shake. You
are disarmed!"

Regrets
Reveries, Changing Skies

"So the poet's habit of living should be set on a key so low
that the common influences should delight him. His cheerfulness should be the gift of the sunlight; the air should
suffice for his inspiration, and he should be tipsy with
water."

—EMERSON

I

The Tuileries

IN THE GARDEN of the Tuileries, the sun this morning fell asleep on each of the stone steps one after
the other, like a blond boy whose light slumber a
passing shadow at once disturbs. Against the old palace walls young sprouts show green. The breath of the
charmed breeze, with the perfume of the past, mingles the scent of lilacs. Statues, that on our public
squares are as terrifying as madwomen, here in the
shrubbery dream like sages under the luminous foliage sheltering their whiteness. The water basins, in
whose depths the blue sky lies basking, shine like eyes.
From the terrace by the water, one can see on the

other bank, coming out of the old quarter of the Quai d'Orsay, as out of another age, a hussar passing by.

A tangle of morning glories overflows the vases crowned with geraniums. The incense of the heliotrope burns in the heat of the sun. In front of the Louvre hollyhocks shoot up, delicate as masts, noble and graceful as columns, blushing like young girls. Iridescent with sun and sighing with love, the water jets rise toward the sky. At the end of the terrace a stone horseman, going at a furious gallop without changing place, lips glued to a joyous trumpet, incarnates all the ardor of the spring.

But now the sky darkens, it is going to rain. The basins, no longer shining with azure, seem like sightless eyes or vases full of tears. The absurd water jet, whipped by the breeze, faster and faster raises toward the sky its now derisory hymn. There is an infinite sadness in the useless sweetness of the lilacs. And over there against the darkening sky, launched at full speed, his marble feet in a motionless and furious movement, urging his charger to a vertiginous gallop, the unconscious cavalier goes on blowing his trumpet forever.

II

Versailles

"A canal that makes even the most inveterate talkers begin to dream the moment they approach it, and where I, whether I am joyous, whether I am sad, am always happy."
—*Letter from* BALZAC *to* M. DE LAMOTTE-AIGRON

EXHAUSTED autumn, that the meager sun no longer warms, loses its last colors one by one. The extreme brightness of its foliage, which has been flaming all through the afternoons, and even mornings, giving the glorious illusion of a perpetual sunset, is extinguished now. Alone the dahlias, the Indian pinks and the yellow violet, white and pink chrysanthemums still shine against autumn's dark and desolate face. At six o'clock in the evening walking through the Tuileries, all bare and gray under an equally somber sky, where the black trees, branch by branch, mark their delicate and deep despair, suddenly a clump stands out with its autumn flowers richly gleaming in the obscurity, and our eyes, accustomed to those ashen gray horizons, are startled by a violent and voluptuous delight. The morning hours are softer now. Occasionally the sun comes out, and having left the terrace by the water, on the great stairway in front of me I can still see my shadow descending the stone steps one by one. I hesitate, after so many others, to say,

"Versailles,"* great name, rusty and sweet, royal cemetery of foliage, of vast waters, and of statues, a truly
aristocratic and demoralizing place where we are not
even troubled by remorse that the lives of so many
workmen should have served only to refine and increase, not so much the joys of another age, as the
melancholy of ours. After so many years, I hesitate to
pronounce your name, and yet how often have I gone
to drink from the ruddy cup of your pink marble
fountains, drink to the drugs, to delirium, the intoxicating and bitter sweetness of those last autumn days.
The earth, mixed with withered leaves and rotted
leaves, from a distance always seemed like a tarnished
mosaic, yellow and violet. As I passed the *Hameau*,
turning up my coat collar, I would hear the cooing of
the doves and everywhere was the intoxicating smell
of boxwood like the odor of Palm Sunday. How was it
that I still could pick a little spring bouquet in the
gardens already sacked by autumn? On the waters the
wind ruffled the petals of a shivering rose. In the universal defoliation around the Trianon, alone the slender arch of a little bridge of white geraniums lifted
its flowers above the icy water with heads bowed ever
so little by the wind. It is true that since I inhaled the
sea breeze and the salty air over Normandy's sunken
roads, and saw the sea gleaming through the flowering
rhododendrons, I know all that the propinquity of
water can add to the charm of vegetation. But how

* And particularly after MM. Maurice Barrés, Henri de Régnier,
Robert de Montesquiou-Fezensac.

much more virginal the purity of this gentle white geranium leaning with gracious modesty over the chilly waters between their banks of dead leaves. O silvery old age of the still green wood, O mournful branches, pools and water-basins that a pious hand has set down here and there like funeral urns offered to the bereavement of the trees!

--------- III ---------

A Walk

IN SPITE of the sky so pure and the sun already warm, the wind blew as cold, the trees were as bare as in winter. To make a fire I had to cut one of those branches I thought was dead, and the sap spurted out, wetting my arm up to the elbow, revealing beneath the tree's icy bark a tumultuous heart. Between the trunks the bare winter earth was being covered with anemones, crocuses and violets; the rivers, yesterday still black and empty, were filled with the tender blue and living sky basking in their depths. Not that pale and languorous sky of lovely autumn evenings which, stretching out along the bottom of the water, seems to be dying there of love and melancholy, but an intense and ardent sky through whose tender laughing azure kept hurrying by, gray, blue and pink, not the shadows of pensive clouds, but the brilliant gliding fins of a perch or eel or sparling. Drunk with joy, they swam between their sky and grasses in their prairies and beneath their hedges which, like ours, had been enchanted by the genie of the spring. And gliding coolly over their heads, between their gills, under their bellies, the waters hurried too, singing and merrily chasing the sunbeams before them.

The barnyard, where one went for eggs, was a no less pleasing sight. The sun, like an inspired and prolific poet who does not scorn to dispense beauty in the humblest places which no one had ever dreamed of including in the realm of art before, warmed the salutary vigor of the dunghill, of the rough paved court, and of the pear tree broken and bent like an old serving woman.

But what is that regally attired personage carefully picking his way among the rustic farm implements as though afraid of soiling his feet, offended by the dirt? It is Juno's bird, gorgeous, not with lifeless gems, but with the eyes of Argus himself, the peacock, whose fabulous splendor seems so surprising in such a place. Just as on some festive occasion, a few moments before the arrival of the first guest, the mistress of the house, in a gown with iridescent train, an azure collaret around her regal throat, resplendent, crosses the courtyard before the marveling eyes of the gapers crowding around the gate, going to give a final order, or to await the arrival of the prince of royal blood whom she must needs greet on the very threshold of her domain.

And yet, it is right here that the peacock spends his life, a veritable bird of paradise in the barnyard among the turkeys and the hens, like a captive Andromache spinning her wool among her slaves, except that unlike her he has left behind none of the splendors of royal insignia and crown jewels, a radiant Apollo, recognizable always—even when he guards Admetus' flocks.

——————————— **IV** ———————————

Family Listening to Music

> "For sweet is music,
> And soothes the soul, and like a heavenly chorus
> Awakes a thousand singing voices in the heart."

FOR A really alert family in which each one thinks, loves, is fully occupied, to have a garden is a pleasant thing. There, on spring, summer and autumn evenings, when the day's tasks are done, they all unite; and no matter how small the garden is, no matter how close its hedges, they are never so high that a little bit of sky is not visible to which each one lifts his eyes full of dreams. The little boy dreams of his plans for the future, of the house he is going to live in with his best friend, never to be separated from him again, of all that earth and life hold for him of the unknown; the young man dreams of the mysterious charm of the girl he loves; the young mother of her child's future; and the woman, unhappy until now, discovers in these luminous hours, beneath her husband's cold demeanor, a hidden pain that fills her now with pity. The

father, watching the smoke rising above the roof,
muses over peaceful scenes out of his past, seen in the
far away enchantment of the evening light; he thinks
of his approaching death, of the life of his children
after his death; and thus the united soul of the whole
family rises religiously toward the setting sun, while
the big linden, walnut, or pine tree sheds over them,
like a benediction, its exquisite fragrance or its vener-
able shade.

But for a really alert family in which each one
thinks, loves, is fully occupied, for a family that has
a soul, how much sweeter even for that soul on summer evenings to become incarnate in the clear and inexhaustible voice of a young girl or of a young man
who has been granted the gift of music and of song.
A stranger, passing by the garden where the family
sits silent, would hesitate to approach for fear of breaking the spell of what seems like a religious dream. But
if the stranger, without hearing any voice singing,
should see the assembled members of the family and
their friends listening, he would be even more convinced that he was assisting at a silent mass; that is, in
spite of the diversity of attitudes, the similarity of
their expressions would reveal the true unity of their
souls, momentarily realized in their sympathy for the
same ideal drama, in their communion in the same
dream. At moments, just as the wind bends the grass
and lingeringly stirs the branches, a breath suddenly
bows or lifts their heads. Then all of them, as though
an invisible messenger were relating some thrilling

story, seem to be anxiously awaiting, listening with transport or with terror to the same piece of news which yet in each awakes such different echoes. The anguish of the music has reached its height, its flights are broken by deep descents followed by more desperate flights. For the old man its luminous infinity, its mysterious shadows, seem to be vast spectacles of life and death, for the boy they are the immediate promises of all the earth and sea, for the lover they are the mysterious infinity and luminous shadows of love. The thinker sees his whole moral life unrolling; the falls of the failing melody are his own falls and his own failings, and his whole heart is uplifted and leaps when the melody again takes flight, the powerful murmurs of the harmonies stir the obscure and profound depths of his memory. The man of action grows breathless in the clashing of the chords, the gallop of the *vivace*, triumphs majestically in the adagios. Even the unfaithful wife feels her sin pardoned, infinitized, a sin which also had its celestial origin in the dissatisfaction of a heart that ordinary joys could not appease, gone astray, it is true, but only because it was searching for the mystery, and whose vast aspirations this music with the voice of churchly bells now satisfies. The musician, too, although pretending that he takes a purely technical pleasure in music, feels these significant emotions, but so shrouded in his concept of beauty that they are hidden from him. And finally, I myself, hearing in music the vastest, most universal beauty of life and of death, of sky and sea, feel, besides, all that your charm holds of particular and unique, O dear Beloved.

────────────────── V ──────────────────

THE paradoxes of today are the prejudices of tomorrow, since the most benighted and the most deplorable prejudices have had their moment of novelty when fashion lent them its fragile grace. Many women today want to be freed of all the prejudices, and by prejudices they mean principles. That is their prejudice, and a heavy one, even though they wear it like a delicate and somewhat exotic flower. For them perspective does not exist; everything is on the same plane. They enjoy a book or life itself as they enjoy an orange or a sunny day. They speak of the "art" of the dressmaker and the "philosophy" of "Parisian life." They would blush to classify anything, to judge anything, to say: "This is good, this is bad." Formerly when a woman behaved properly it was the triumph of her morality, that is, of her mind over her instinctive nature. Today when a woman behaves properly it is the triumph of her instinctive nature over her morality, or rather over her theoretic immorality. In the extreme slackness of all moral and social restraints, women float between this theoretic immorality and their instinctive rectitude. They look only for pleasure and find it only when they are not looking for it, when they accept suffering. In books such skepticism and dilettantism would seem as shocking as an outmoded gown. But women, far from being the oracles of intellectual fashions, are rather the belated parrots. Even today dilettantism still pleases and becomes them. And even if it warps their judgment, makes their behavior ineffectual, one cannot deny that it lends them a particular grace, withered now but still alluring. They make us blissfully feel how easy life could be in an ultra-refined civilization, and how sweet. Their perpetual departure for a spiritual Cytherea, where the festivities would appeal less to their dulled senses than to their imagination, heart, mind, eyes, nose and ears, lends some special voluptuousness to their poses. And I suppose that the most exact portrait painter today would hardly show them with anything very stiff or prim about them. Their life diffuses a perfume as pleasant as the scent of floating hair.

VI

AMBITION is more intoxicating than fame; desire makes all things flourish, possession withers them; it is better to dream one's life than to live it, although in living life one dreams it still, but less mysteriously and at the same time less vividly, as in an obscure and sluggish dream, like the diffused dream in the feeble consciousness of a ruminating animal. Shakespeare's plays are more beautiful seen in our studies than on the stage. Most of the poets who have created immortal lovers themselves knew nothing more sublime than the love of barmaids, while the most envied

voluptuaries have no conception of the life they lead,
or rather that leads them. I once knew a little boy of
ten, with precarious health and a precocious imagination, who had conceived for a little girl older than
himself a purely intellectual passion. He would stand
in front of his window for hours to see her pass, would
weep if he did not see her, would weep even more bit-
terly if he did. He spent rare and very brief moments
with her. He could no longer eat or sleep. One day he
threw himself out of the window. At first everyone
thought that despair at never seeing his love had
made him decide to die. But on the contrary, it was
discovered that he had just had a long conversation
with her and that she had been extremely kind to
him. Then it was supposed that after the intoxication
which he would perhaps never know again, he could
not face the insipidity of the days to come. However,
from one of his friends in whom at one time he had
frequently confided, it was learned that he always felt
a keen disappointment every time he saw the sovereign of his dreams, but that the moment she was out
of sight his fertile imagination would invest the absent little girl with all her former power, and he
would long to see her again. And each time he would
try to find in some fault of circumstance the reason
for his disappointment. After this final interview,
when with the help of his precocious imagination he
had led his little sweetheart to the highest perfection
of which her nature was capable, comparing that imperfect perfection with the absolute perfection by

which he lived and by which he died, he had in despair thrown himself from the window. Afterwards, a hopeless idiot, he lived for many years, but having lost in his fall all remembrance of his soul, his mind and the voice of his little sweetheart, whom he no longer knew. And she, in spite of prayers and menaces, insisted on marrying him, and died years later without his ever having recognized her. Life is like this little sweetheart. We dream of it and we love it in dreaming of it. But we must not try to live it. Like the little boy we throw ourselves into stupidity, not all at once, for in life everything is degraded gradually and by imperceptible degrees. After ten years we no longer recognize our dreams, or else we disown them, and we live like an ox for whatever grass we find to graze on at the moment. And who knows, perhaps from our wedding with death will be born our conscious immortality!

VII

"Captain," said his orderly a few days after the little house was ready where, now that he had been retired, he was to live until his death (which a heart ailment would not keep waiting long), "Captain, perhaps now that you can't make love any more or fight, you might like to read. What books shall I buy for you?"

"None. Buy no books; they can have nothing to relate more interesting than the things I have done, and since I have such a little time left I want nothing to distract me from my memories. Give me the key to my large chest; in it there is plenty for me to read every day."

And he began taking letters out of it, a whitish and sometimes tinted sea of letters, very long letters, letters of a single line, on calling cards, with faded flowers, objects with little notes in his own handwriting attached to them to remind him of everything connected with the moment they had been received, photographs, dilapidated in spite of all his precautions, having been kissed too often like relics worn away by the very piety of the faithful. And all these things dated from very long ago, and there were those of women who were now dead, others he had not seen for ten years or more.

There were, in all this, precise little things made up of sensuality or tenderness connected with the most trifling circumstances of his life, and it was like a vast fresco, painting his life without relating it, and only in its most passionate colors, in a vague and at the same time a very particular manner, with touching power. There were reminders of kisses on a mouth —a fresh young mouth where he would willingly have left his soul, and which since had turned away from him—had caused him many tears. And although he was weak now and without hope, when like a glass of warming wine ripened in the sun he emptied in one gulp some of these still living memories that had consumed his life, he felt a warm, agreeable shiver such as spring brings to our convalescences and winter

hearthfires to our weaknesses. The feeling that his old
worn body had once burned with such a flame was
like a renewal of life for him—burned with such de-
vouring flames. Then, thinking that all these things
hovering around him still were, alas! only enormous
and moving shadows, impossible to grasp and which
would soon be confounded all together in the eternal
night, he began to weep again.

And yet, knowing all the while that they were only
shadows, shadows of flames now gone to burn elsewhere that he would never see again, he began to
adore these shadows and to lend them, as it were, a
cherished existence in contrast to the absolute oblivion soon to come. And all these things—all these kisses
and all these much kissed locks of hair, and things
made up of tears and lips, caresses poured out like
wine to intoxicate, and of despairs swelling like music or like evening, for the joy of being filled to infinitude with mystery and destiny; and a certain Adored
One who had possessed him so utterly that nothing
had existed for him but that which fed his adoration,
who had possessed him utterly and now escaped him,
so vague he could no longer hold her back, not even
the perfume floating out of the folds of her vanishing
cloak—he made a desperate effort to recapture them,
to resuscitate and nail them up before him like
mounted butterflies. And it became more difficult
each time. And not one of these butterflies had he
ever caught, but had only rubbed a little of the mirage
off their wings each time; or rather he saw them as in

a mirror and, vainly trying to touch them, had succeeded only in blurring the glass a little more each time, saw them only indistinctly and less charming. And this tarnished mirror of his heart, now that the cleansing breath of youth or of genius would pass over him no more, nothing could wipe clear—through what unknown law of our human seasons, by what mysterious equinox of our autumns. . . .

And each time he felt less sorrow to have lost them, those kisses of that mouth, and those infinite hours, and those once intoxicating perfumes.

And he suffered now in suffering less. Then his sufferings departed, all of them, but nothing was needed to make his pleasures depart; they had fled long ago on their winged feet, averting their faces and holding flowering branches in their hands, fled from this dwelling no longer young enough for them. Then, like all other men, he died.

VIII

Relics

I BOUGHT everything that had belonged to her, whose lover I had longed to be, and who had refused to speak to me even for an instant. I have the little pack of cards that entertained her every evening, her two *ouistitis*, her dog and three novels that bear her coat of arms. O you delights and perished pastimes of her life, you who, without relishing them as I should have done, without even having sought them, were privileged to know her freest hours, her most inviolable and secret hours, you never felt your happiness and cannot now relate it.

Cards that her fingers handled every evening with her closest friends, that saw her bored or in her merry moods, that were present when her liaison first began, when she flung you aside to kiss the one who came to be her partner every evening after that; novels that she would open when she went to bed or close again according to her fancy or fatigue, that she chose following the whim of the moment or her dreams in which she confided, and that mixed their dreams with hers, helping her better to dream her own, have you kept nothing of her, is there nothing you can tell?

You, her novels, because in her turn she dreamed of the life of your characters and of your author; you, her cards, because with you in her own way she felt the calm and at times the fever of living intimacies, have you retained nothing of her mind which you entertained and filled, of her heart you opened and consoled?

Cards, novels, since you have been so often in her hands, lain so long upon her table, queens, kings or knaves who were the silent guests of all her gayest parties; heroes of her novels, and heroines, who, beside her bed in the crossing rays of her lamp and of her eyes, would dream your silent dream yet filled with voices, can it be that all the perfumes with which you were impregnated by the air of her room, the tissues of her gowns, the touch of her hands or of her knees, have all been dissipated? You have kept the creases with which her joyous or nervous hands had marked you; perhaps the tears which, for a fictive sorrow or a real one, her eyes once shed, you still hold prisoner; and perhaps your warm color came to you the day that made her eyes so bright or made them sad. I touch you tremblingly, waiting for your revelations, troubled by your silence. Alas! like you, charming and fragile creatures, she may have been an insensible and unconscious witness of her own grace. Her most genuine beauty was perhaps in my desire. She lived her life, but I alone perhaps have dreamed it.

IX

Moonlight Sonata

I.

MORE than the fatigues of walking, the memory and dread of my father's severity, Pia's indifference and the animosity of my enemies had exhausted me. During the day Assunta's presence, her singing, her sweetness to me, of which she was so little aware, her white and brown and pink coolness, her perfume that lingered in the gusts of wind from the sea, the feather in her hat, the pearls around her throat, had served to cheer me. But toward nine o'clock in the evening, feeling oppressed, I asked her to return in the carriage and leave me to rest awhile in the open air. We had nearly reached Honfleur; the place was well chosen against a wall, at the entrance of a double row of tall trees serving as a protection from the wind, the air was mild. She assented and left me. I lay down on the grass, my face turned toward the somber sky, soothed by the noise of the ocean that I could hear behind me but could not see in the dusk. It was not long before I fell asleep.

Soon I dreamed that in front of me the setting sun was lighting up the sand and the sea in the distance. Twilight was falling and it seemed to me that it was a sunset and a twilight like all other twilights and sunsets. But someone brought me a letter; I tried to read it and was unable to make out the words. It was only then I noticed that in spite of the sensation of intense and diffused light, it was very dark. This sunset was extraordinarily pale, luminous without light, and on the sand thus magically illuminated, the darkness was so dense that I had to make an effort to recognize a shell. In this twilight, characteristic of dreams, it was like the setting of a sick and colorless sun on some polar beach. My worries had suddenly flown; my father's decisions, Pia's preferences, my enemies' bad faith were still predominant but no longer crushing, like a natural necessity one was able to ignore. The contradiction of this dark resplendency, the miracle of this enchanted suspension of my ills, awoke in me not the least distrust nor any dread, but I was enveloped, bathed, drowned in an ever increasing bliss whose delicious intensity finally awakened me. I opened my eyes. Glorious and pale my dream spread all around me. The wall against which I had leaned to rest was in full light, and the shadow of the ivy covering it as sharp as at four o'clock in the afternoon. The leaves of a silver poplar sparkled as an imperceptible breeze turned them one by one. On the water white waves and sails were visible, the sky was clear, the moon had risen. At times light clouds passed over it, but were straightway covered with bluish tints whose pallor was as profound as that of the gelatinous medusa or as the heart of an opal. But nowhere could my eyes locate the light that shone everywhere. And masses of darkness lay even over the grass, as resplendent as a mirage. The woods, a ditch, were absolutely black. All at once a slight noise, beginning lingeringly like a feeling of distress, quickly swelled and seemed to roll over the woods. It was the shivering of the leaves ruffled by the wind. One by one I could hear them lapping like waves on the vast silence of the night. Then even this sound diminished and disappeared. In the narrow meadow stretching before me between the two thick rows of oak trees, a river of light seemed to be flowing, confined between its two banks of shadow. The light of the moon in summoning up out of the night the keeper's lodge, the foliage, a sail, had not awakened them. In this silence of sleep it lighted only the vague phantom of their forms so that I could not distinguish their contours which during the day made them so real for me, oppressed me with the certainty of their presence, and with the persistence of their commonplace proximity. The house without a door, the foliage without a tree, almost without leaves, the sail without a boat, seemed, rather than a cruel reality, undeniable and monotonously ordinary, like the strange dream, unstable and luminous, of the sleeping trees that were plunged in darkness. Never, indeed, had the woods slept so profoundly; one felt that the moon had taken advantage of their unconsciousness to inaugurate, without a sound in sky and sea, this vast celebration, lovely and pale. My sadness had vanished. I listened to my father scolding me, Pia laughing at me, my enemies contriving their plots, and it all seemed to me unreal. The only reality was this unreal light, and smiling I turned to it. I did not understand what mysterious resemblance united my sorrows and these solemn mysteries that were being celebrated in the woods and in the sky and on the sea, but I felt that they were proffering their explanation, their consolation, their pardon, and that it did not in the least matter that my mind had no part in the secret since my heart understood it so well. I called by name my holy mother, the Night. My sadness had recognized in the moon its immortal sister. The moon shone on the transfigured sorrows of the night and in my heart, where the clouds had been dispersed, my melancholy lifted.

II.

Then I heard footsteps. Assunta was coming toward me, her white face rising out of a voluminous dark cloak. She said almost in a whisper: "I was afraid you

would be cold; my brother was in bed, I came back."
I went up to her, I shivered; she took me under her
cloak and, to keep the folds about me, put her arm
around my neck. We walked a few paces under the
trees in complete darkness. Something shone in our
path. I had no time to draw back and tried to step
aside, thinking we were about to run into a tree, but
the obstacle gave way under our feet; we had walked
in a piece of the moon. I drew her head close to mine.
She smiled, and I began to weep. I saw that she was
weeping too. Then we knew that the moon was weeping and that its sadness was in tune with ours. The
sweet and poignant accents of its light pierced our
hearts. Like us she was weeping and, as is usually the
case with us, was weeping without knowing why, but
with such profound emotion that she had inspired
with her own sweet and irresistible despair woods,
fields and sky, which were now once more reflected in
the sea, as well as in my heart that saw clearly into my
heart at last.

X

Source of the Tears Contained in Former Loves

THE REPININGS of novelists and their heroes over their
dead loves, so touching for the reader, are unfortu-
nately entirely artificial. This contrast between the
immensity of our former love and the absoluteness of
our present indifference, of which we are made con-

scious by a thousand details—a name mentioned in conversation, a letter discovered in a drawer, even meeting the person herself or, better still, possessing her again but, as it were, too late—this contrast so afflicting, so full of tears in a work of art, we, in real life, observe insensibly, precisely because our present state is one of indifference and oblivion, because our beloved and our love appeal to us no longer, except perhaps aesthetically, and because with love our anxiety, our faculty for suffering have disappeared. The poignant melancholy of this contrast is then a moral truth only. It would become a psychological reality too if a writer were to place it at the beginning of the passion he is describing, instead of at the end.

Indeed, it often happens that when we begin to be in love, warned by our experience and our common sense—in spite of the protestation of our heart, which has the conviction, or rather the illusion, of our love's eternity—we know that the woman by the thought of whom we live will be as indifferent to us as are now all those others except herself. We shall hear her name spoken without the least thrill of pain, shall see her handwriting without trembling, we shall not go out of our way to catch a glimpse of her in the street, we shall meet her without emotion, possess her without delirium. And this foresight, in spite of our absurd but irresistible prepossession that we shall love her forever, makes us weep. And love, love that will once more have risen over us like a divine dawn infinitely mysterious and sad, will spread out before our grief something of its own vast and strange horizons, something of its own bewitching desolation. . . .

—————————— XI ——————————

Friendship

IT IS comforting when one has a sorrow to lie in the warmth of one's bed and there, abandoning all effort and all resistance, to bury even one's head under the cover, giving one's self up to it completely, moaning like branches in the autumn wind. But there is a still better bed, full of divine odors. It is our sweet, our profound, our impenetrable friendship. When sad and cold, that is where I lay my chilly heart. Burying even my mind in our warm tenderness, seeing nothing else, defending myself no longer, disarmed, but through the miracle of our tenderness straightway strengthened invincible. I weep for my sorrow and for joy at having a place of trust where I can hide it.

—————————— XII ——————————

Ephemeral Efficacy of Sorrow

LET US be grateful to people who make us happy; they are the charming gardeners who make our souls blossom. But let us be even more grateful to unkind or only indifferent women, to cruel friends who have caused us sorrow. They have devastated our heart, which is now scattered all over with unrecognizable debris; they have, like a devastating wind, uprooted trunks and mutilated the most delicate branches, but they have sown a few good seeds for an uncertain harvest.

In cutting down all our little joys that hid our wretchedness, in making of our heart a bare and melancholy playground, they have enabled us to see it plainly at last and to judge it. Sad plays are good for us in the same way, and consequently should be considered far superior to gay ones, which beguile our hunger without satisfying it; the bread that nourishes is bitter. When life is happy the fate of our fellow-creatures does not appear in its true light, either masked by self-interest or transformed by desire. But in the detachment that in life comes to us with suffering, and from the sensation of sorrowful beauty on the stage, the fate of other men and even our own awakes our soul at last, the unheeded and eternal voice of duty and of truth. The sad works of a true artist speak to us in the tone of those who have suffered, making all men who have suffered cast everything else aside to listen.

Alas! What capricious feeling gives one day, it takes away the next, and sadness, nobler than gaiety, is not, like virtue, steadfast. This morning we have forgotten the tragedy that last night raised us so that we could see our life in its entirety and truth with a clairvoyant and sincere compassion. But in a year, perhaps, a woman's betrayal, the death of a friend will be forgotten. The wind in all this noise of dreams, this litter of withered joys, has sown the good seed under a shower of tears, but tears which will have dried before the seed can germinate.

(After the Invitée of M. de Curel)

─────────────── XIII ───────────────

In Praise of Bad Music

DETEST BAD music but do not despise it. As it is played, and especially sung, much more passionately than good music, it has much more than the latter been impregnated, little by little, with man's tears. Hold it therefore in veneration. Its place, nonexistent in the history of art, is immense in the sentimental history of nations. The respect—I do not say love—for bad music is not only a form of what might be called the charity of good taste, or its skepticism; it is also the consciousness of the importance of music's social role. How many tunes, worthless in the eyes of an artist, are numbered among the chosen confidants of a multitude of romantic young men and girls in love. How many *"bague d'or,"* how many *"Ah! reste longtemps endormi,"* whose pages are turned tremblingly every evening by hands justly famous, drenched with the tears of the most beautiful eyes in the world,

whose melancholy and voluptuous tribute would be
the envy of the purest musicians—ingenious and inspired confidants that ennoble sorrow and exalt
dreams and, in exchange for the ardent secret confided to them, give the intoxicating illusion of beauty.
The people, the bourgeoisie, the army, the nobility,
all of them, just as they have the same mail carriers,
purveyors of afflicting sorrow or of crowning joy,
have the same invisible messengers of love, the same
cherished confessors. Bad musicians, certainly. Some
miserable ritournelle that every well-born and well-
trained ear instantly refuses to listen to receives the
tribute of millions of souls, guards the secret of millions of lives for whom it has been the living inspiration, the ever ready consolation always open on the
piano-rack, the dreamy charm and the ideal. Certain
arpeggios, a certain "rentrée" have made the soul of
many a lover vibrate with the harmonies of Paradise
or the voice of the beloved herself. A collection of bad
Romances worn with constant use should touch us
as a cemetery touches us, or a village. What does it
matter if the houses have no style, if the tombstones
are hidden by inscriptions and ornaments in ex-
ecrable taste? Before an imagination sympathetic and
respectful enough to silence for a moment its aesthetic
scorn, from this dust that flock of souls may rise
holding in their beaks the still verdant dream which
has given them a foretaste of the other world, and
made them rejoice or weep in this one.

—————————— XIV ——————————

Encounter by the Lake

YESTERDAY, before going to a dinner in the Bois, I received a note from Her, in which after eight days she replied quite coldly to my desperate letter that she was afraid she would be unable to see me before she left. And I, quite coldly, yes, I replied that it was perhaps just as well, and that I wished her a pleasant summer. I then dressed and, in an open carriage, drove through the Bois. I was excessively sad, but calm. I had determined to forget her, I had made up my mind; it was a question of time.

As the carriage turned into the lake drive I noticed, at the far end of the little path that circles the lake about fifty yards or more distant from the drive, a woman alone, walking along slowly. I did not see her clearly at first. She greeted me with a little wave of her hand, and then, in spite of the distance that separated us, I recognized her. It was She! I made her a low bow. And she continued to look at me as though wanting me to take her with me. I did nothing of the sort, but, almost at once, I felt an emotion that was like something exterior to myself swoop down and take possession of me. "I have always known it!" I cried to myself. "There is some reason unknown to me that has made her affect indifference. Dear heart, she loves me." An infinite happiness, an invincible certainty invaded me. I felt as though I were about to

faint; I burst out sobbing. The carriage was nearing
Armenonville. I wiped my eyes, and that gentle waving hand, as though wishing to dry them too, passed
over them, and her softly questioning eyes, still fixed
on mine, seemed to be asking me to take her with me.

I arrived at the dinner party exultant. My happiness poured over everyone in joyous amiability, grateful and cordial, and the feeling that no one had the
least idea what hand, unknown to them—the little
hand that had waved to me—had kindled this joyous
bonfire in my heart, whose radiant effect anyone
could see, added the charm of a secret pleasure to my
happiness. We were now only waiting for Madame
de T . . ., who soon arrived. She is the most insignificant person I know, and although she has rather
a good figure, the most unattractive. But I was so
happy I forgave her all her faults, even her ugliness,
and smiling went up to her with an affectionate air.

"Just now you were much less amiable," she said.

"Just now!" I replied in astonishment. "Just now?
But I have not seen you before."

"What! You didn't recognize me then? It's true, you
were quite a distance away. I was walking by the lake
when you sailed proudly by in your carriage. I waved
to you and, as I was late, I hoped that you would stop
and take me with you."

"You mean that it was you!" I cried, and despair-
ingly several times repeated, "Oh, do forgive me, do
please forgive me."

"How miserable he looks! I congratulate you, Charlotte. But you must cheer up now, since she is with you."

I was overwhelmed; my happiness had been annihilated.

But the most horrible part of it was that the truth had failed to obliterate what had never been. That loving image of the woman who did not love me, even now that I was aware of my mistake, completely, and for a long time, changed my whole conception of her. I attempted a reconciliation; I was unable to forget her as I might otherwise have done, and often for consolation in my suffering, and making believe that they were really hers as I had *felt* that day, I would close my eyes to see once more the little hands that had waved to me, that would have dried my eyes and cooled my brow, those little gloved hands she had held out to me by the lake-side, frail symbols of peace, of love, and reconciliation, while her sad questioning eyes had seemed to be asking me to take her with me.

─────────────── XV ───────────────

As THE blood-red sky warns the passer-by: there is a fire over there, so certain fiery glances reveal passions which they merely reflect. They are flames in the looking-glass. But often, too, the eyes of the gayest and most carefree persons are large and dark with every sorrow, as though a filter, held between their soul and their eyes, had "strained" out all the living content of the soul. After that, **warmed** only by the fervor of their own egotism—that irresistible fervor of egotism which attracts people as strongly as the conflagration of passion repels them—their withered soul will henceforth be but the unreal palace of intrigues. But their eyes, endlessly kindled by love, which a languorous dew waters, makes lustrous and vague, drowns but never extinguishes, will continue to amaze the universe with their tragic blaze. Twin spheres henceforth severed from the soul, spheres of love, ardent satellites of a world extinct forever, will continue until death to throw out an unwonted and unwarranted refulgence, false prophets and perjuries, that give the promise of a love their heart will fail to keep.

XVI

The Stranger

DOMINIQUE was sitting in front of the dying fire waiting for his guests to arrive. Every evening he invited some great nobleman to sup with him in the company of men of wit, and as he was well-born, rich and charming, he was never alone. The candles had not been lighted and in the room the day was sadly dying. All at once he heard a voice saying, a far-away and intimate voice saying: "Dominique," and only to hear the way it uttered, uttered from so far away and yet so close, "Dominique," froze him with fear. Never had he heard that voice, and yet he recognized it perfectly;

his remorse recognized perfectly the voice of a victim, of a noble victim sacrificed by him. He tried to recall some former crime he had committed and could remember none. Yet the tone of that voice, which was certainly reproaching him for a crime, a crime he had committed, no doubt unconsciously, but for which he was responsible, betrayed its sadness and anxiety. He raised his eyes and saw standing before him, very grave and familiar, a stranger with a vague and striking air. Dominique acknowledged in a few respectful words his evident and melancholy authority.

"Dominique, am I to be the only one not invited to your supper?"

"But I do invite you to my supper," said Dominique with a grave warmth that surprised him.

"Thank you," said the stranger.

No crest was inscribed on his signet ring, nor had wit frosted his speech with its sparkling needles, but the gratitude that shone in his firm and fraternal gaze thrilled Dominique with a novel happiness.

"But if you wish me to stay, you must send the other guests away."

Dominique could hear them knocking on the door. The candles were not yet lighted, the room was in total darkness.

"I cannot send them away," replied Dominique. *"I cannot bear to be alone."*

"It is true," said the stranger sadly, "with me you would be alone. Yet, for all that, you should let me stay with you. There are old wrongs you have done me, wrongs you should repair. I love you more than they do, those others who, when you are old, will come to you no longer."

"I cannot," said Dominique.

And at the same moment he felt that he had sacrificed a noble happiness for a tyrannical and vulgar habit and one, besides, which, in return for his obedience, had no more pleasures to offer him.

"Choose quickly," said the stranger beseechingly, proudly.

Dominique went to open the door for his guests, at the same time asking the stranger, without daring to turn his head, "But who are you?"

And the stranger—the stranger who had already disappeared—replied, "Habit, to which you sacrifice me this evening, tomorrow, nourished by the blood of the wounds you have inflicted on me, will be stronger than ever. Each day more exigent for having been obeyed again, it will lead you a little farther from me, force you to make me suffer even more. Soon you will have killed me. You will never see me again. Yet you owe more to me than to the others, who will soon desert you. I am within you, yet I am now very far away; I hardly exist any longer. I am your soul, I am yourself."

The guests had entered. They all went to the dining room and Dominique tried to tell them of his interview with the vanished stranger. But Girolomo, observing the general boredom of the guests and his host's difficulty in recalling an almost forgotten dream, to the great satisfaction of everybody including Dominique himself interrupted him, drawing the following conclusion: "One should never remain alone. Solitude begets melancholy."

Then they all began drinking again. Dominique chatted gaily but without joy, flattered by the brilliance of the company.

XVII

A Dream

"You shed your tears for me, my lips have drunk your tears."
—ANATOLE FRANCE

I HAVE no difficulty in recalling what my opinion of Madame Dorothy B . . . was on Saturday (four days ago). It chanced that on that day her name was mentioned, and I was perfectly sincere in saying that for me she was without the least wit or charm. I think she is twenty-two or -three. As a matter of fact I hardly knew her; no vivid image rose to my mind when I thought of her, but only the letters of her name stood out before my eyes.

Saturday night I went to bed rather early. But toward two o'clock, a wind having risen, I was forced to get up to close a badly fastened shutter that had waked me. I thought of the brief sleep I had just enjoyed, and felt delighted that it had been so restful, invigorating, free from distress and without dreams. I was hardly back in bed again before I fell asleep.

But after a little while, how long it is impossible to say, I began gradually waking again, or rather, little by little I woke into the world of dreams, blurred at first, like the real world when we first awake, but which soon became distinct. I was lying on the beach at Trouville which, at the same time, was a hammock in a garden I had never seen before, and a woman was looking at me with an intent and tender gaze. It was Madame Dorothy B. . . . I was no more surprised to see her than I am in the morning when I open my eyes to recognize my room. Nor was I surprised by the supernatural charm of my companion, nor by the transports of voluptuous and spiritual adoration that her presence caused me. We looked at each other with perfect understanding, and there was a great miracle of happiness and exultation occurring of which we were both conscious, she being in some way responsible for it, and I filled with infinite gratitude toward her.

"You are mad to thank me; would you not have done the same thing for me?"

And the idea (as a matter of fact it was an absolute certainty) that I should have done the same thing for her made me delirious with joy, as the symbol of the closeness of our union. She made a mysterious sign with her finger and smiled. And I knew, as though I had been both in her and in myself at the same time, that this meant: Do they matter any longer, all your enemies, all your misfortunes, all your regrets and all your weaknesses? And without

my saying a word she heard me reply that she had
easily triumphed over all of them, destroyed them all,
voluptuously mesmerized my suffering, and she came
nearer, caressed my neck with her hands, slowly
lifted the ends of my mustache. Then she said: "Now
let us go to the others, let us enter life." I was filled
with a superhuman joy, and felt that I had strength
enough to realize all this virtual happiness. She
wanted to give me a flower; drew from between her
breasts a half opened rose, yellow and faintly pink,
and put it in my buttonhole. All at once I felt my intoxication redoubled by a new voluptuousness. It
was the rose in my buttonhole under my nose that had
begun to exhale its love-scent. I saw that my joy had
moved Dorothy with an emotion I did not understand. At the very moment when her eyes (and because of the mysterious consciousness I had of her
particular individuality, I was sure of it) showed the
light quiver that precedes by an instant the moment
of weeping, it was my eyes that filled with tears, with
her tears I might say. She drew nearer, her head
lifted to the level of my cheeks, her upturned face
allowing me to contemplate its mysterious charm and
captivating vivacity, and darting her tongue out between her dewy lips, smiling she gathered all my tears.
Then she swallowed them with a little noise of her
lips and I felt a mysterious kiss much more intimately
disquieting than if her mouth had actually touched
mine.

Brusquely I woke up, recognized my room and,

just as in a storm not far off a flash of lightning is instantaneously followed by a clap of thunder, a vertiginous recollection of my happiness did not so much precede as become identified with the fulgurating realization of its falsehood and impossibility. But, in spite of all my reasoning, Dorothy B . . . had now ceased to be the woman she had been for me the day before. The faint trace left in my memory by my slight acquaintance with her had almost disappeared, just as a strong tide ebbing leaves strange vestiges behind. Now I had an overwhelming desire, doomed to disappointment in advance, to see her again, an instinctive need of writing to her combined with a more sensible circumspection. The mention of her name in conversation made me tremble, yet evoked only the same insignificant image that would have come to me before that night, and while she meant no more to me than any other ordinary society woman, I yearned toward her more irresistibly than toward the most cherished mistress or the promise of the most intoxicating destiny. I would not have moved a finger to see her and yet for "her," that other one, I would have given my life. With every passing hour the memory of my dream fades a little more, sufficiently distorted, as it is, by this account; I see it less and less clearly, like a book one tries to go on reading at one's table after nightfall when there is no longer enough light. To see it still, I must stop thinking of it now and then, as one has to close one's eyes to make out a letter or two on the shadowy page. All blurred as it is,

it has left a troubled longing in me still, the foam of
its wake, the voluptuousness of its perfume. But if I
were to see Madame B . . . this perturbation would
vanish, and I should meet her without the least emotion. But why should I, after all, speak to her of things
she knows nothing about?

Alas! love has passed over me like my dream, with
just as mysterious a power of transfiguration. But you
who know this woman whom I love, and who were
not present in my dream, you cannot possibly understand. Don't give me your advice.

XVIII

Memory's Genre Paintings

WE HAVE certain memories which might be called our
memory's Dutch School of painting, in which the
people are usually of modest station, caught at some
ordinary moment of their lives, without solemn hap-
penings, often without anything happening at all, in
a setting that is not in the least extraordinary, without grandeur. The whole charm lies in the natural-
ness of the characters and the simplicity of the scene,
remoteness throwing its lovely light between us and
the picture, and bathing it in beauty.

My military life is full of scenes of this sort. I lived
them naturally, without great joy and without great
sorrow, and I remember them with great tenderness.
The rural character of the places, the simplicity of
some of my peasant comrades whose bodies were

more beautiful and more agile, their minds more original, their hearts more spontaneous, their characters more natural than in the case of the young men I had known before, or those I knew afterwards, the peacefulness of a life where one's occupations are more strictly regulated and one's imagination less trammeled than in any other, where pleasure is more constantly present because we have not time in rushing about looking for it to run away from it, all these things concur to make this period of my life a series of little paintings, with many blanks, it is true, but full of a happy reality and a charm over which time has now spread its gentle sadness and its poetry.

———————————— XIX ————————————

Wind of the Sea in the Country

"I will bring you a young poppy with purple petals."
—THEOCRITUS: *The Cyclops*

IN THE garden, in the little wood, across the countryside, the wind with a mad and futile ardor is busy dispersing the gusts of sun and chasing them, with the help of the furiously tossing branches, from the copse where they had first swept down up to the sparkling thicket where all palpitating they are quivering now. In the clear air the trees, the drying linen, the spreading peacock's tail throw blue and extraordinarily sharp shadows that fly before the wind without leaving the ground, like badly launched kites. This pandemonium of wind and light makes this countryside of Champagne seem like the seashore. Surely when we have reached the top of the path, on fire with sun and breathless with wind, that climbs in the full sunlight toward a naked sky, we shall catch a glimpse of the sea, all white with foam and sun?

You had come, as you did every morning, with your hands full of flowers and a few soft feathers that a ring-dove or a swallow or a blue-jay had let fall in its flight. The feathers tremble in my hat, the poppy in my buttonhole sheds its petals—let's hurry home.

The house moans like a ship in the wind, invisible sails can be heard puffing outside, and the clacking of invisible flags. Let this bunch of roses lie in your lap, and let my heart weep in your encompassing hands.

XX

Pearls

IN THE morning I came home and shivering went to bed, shaking with an icy and melancholy fever. A little while ago in your room your friends of the day before, your plans for the day to come—just so many enemies, so many plots contrived against me—the thoughts you had been thinking—so many vague and inaccessible regions—all came between us. Now that I am away from you, that imperfect presence, fugitive mask of eternal absence which kisses so quickly lift, would suffice, it now seems to me, to reveal your true visage and satisfy all the aspirations of my love. It was necessary that I should leave you, that, chilled and sad, I should stay here far away from you! But by means of what sudden spell do the familiar dreams of our happiness, thick smoke of a brightly burning flame, begin once more to rise joyously and steadily in my brain? In my hands, now warmed by the covers, the smell of the rose-scented cigarettes you made me smoke has been revived. My mouth glued to my hand, I drink in the perfume which in the heat of memory exhales great whiffs of tenderness, of happiness, of "you." Ah! my little beloved, now at the very moment when I am able to get along without you, when I float happily in my memory of you—which fills the room at this moment—without having to struggle against your impervious body, I tell you absurdly, I tell you irresistibly, I cannot live without you. It is your presence that gives my life that delicate, melancholy, warm color like the pearls that spend the night around your neck. Like them, I live and change color in the heat of your body and like them, unless you kept me close to you, I should die.

XXI

The Shores of Oblivion

"They say that Death embellishes those he strikes and exaggerates their virtues, but it is rather that life has generally wronged them. Death, that pious and

irreproachable witness, truthfully and charitably
teaches us that in every man there is usually more
good than evil." What Michelet says here of death is
perhaps even truer of that other death which follows
a great and unhappy love. Is it enough to say of the
person who, after having made us suffer, is nothing
to us any longer, that, in the popular phrase, she is
"dead to us"? But we still weep for the dead, we still
love them, and for a long while we are still under the
irresistible spell of their charm that survives them
and keeps us returning often to their graves. On the
contrary, the person for whom there is nothing we
have not suffered, with whose essence we are satu-
rated, is now powerless to cause us even the shadow of
a pain or of a joy. After having held her as the only
precious thing in all the world, after having reviled
her, after having despised her, now we can barely distinguish her features with the eyes of our memory,
dimmed from having gazed on them too fixedly and
too long. But this opinion of our beloved, an opinion
that has so often varied, sometimes torturing our
blind hearts with its clairvoyance and sometimes
blinding itself to put an end to that cruel disaccord,
must now accomplish a final oscillation. Like those
landscapes seen only from the summits, only from the
heights of forgiveness does she appear in her true
light, the one who was more than dead to us after
having been our entire life. We only knew that she
did not return our love; now we understand that she
gave us her true friendship. It is not memory that em-

bellishes her, it is love that had wronged her. For the person who demands all—and obtaining it would still remain unsatisfied—a little can only seem a senseless cruelty. Now we realize what a generous gift it was from her whom all our despair, our irony, our unremitting tyranny could not discourage. She had been invariably kind. Several of her remarks, repeated to us today, seem to us indulgently just and full of charm, remarks of the woman we had believed incapable of understanding us because she did not love us. While we, on the contrary, have talked about her with such selfishness, harshness and injustice! Besides, how much we owe her! While that great tide of love has ebbed forever, yet, strolling through ourselves we can still gather strange and charming sea-shells and lifting them to our ear can hear, with a melancholy pleasure and without suffering, the same mighty roar as in the past. Then we begin to think tenderly of the woman who, to our misfortune, was more loved than loving. She is not "worse than dead" to us. She is someone who is dead and remembered with affection. Justice requires that we should alter our idea of her. And through the omnipotence of justice she is mentally resuscitated in our hearts to hear this final judgment that, far away from her, we render calmly and with eyes full of tears.

———————————— XXII ————————————

Bodily Presence

WE LOVED each other in a village lost in the Engadine, whose name had a twofold loveliness: the reverie of German sonorities died there in the voluptuousness of Italian syllables. Three lakes of an incredible green reflected the pine forests all around. Glaciers and mountain peaks shut in the horizon. And the loveliness of the evening light was multiplied by the diversity of all these different perspectives. Can we ever forget those walks on the shore of Lake Sils-Maria, at six o'clock when afternoon was drawing to a close? The larches of so dark a serenity against the dazzling snow held out over the pale blue—the almost mauve water—their branches of a sleek and brilliant green. One evening the hour was particularly propitious; in a few seconds the setting sun had covered the water with all the colors of the rainbow, our souls with all delights. Suddenly we gave a start; we had just seen a little pink butterfly—then two, then five—leaving the flowers on our shore and fluttering out over the lake. Soon they appeared to us like a rising dust, pink and impalpable. Then they reached the flowers on the opposite shore, started back and began their adventurous crossing once more, stopping at times, as though tempted, above the lake so preciously tinted at this hour like a great flower that is fading. It was too much for us; our eyes filled with tears. These little butterflies crossing the lake passed and repassed over our souls, taut with emotion before so much beauty, ready to vibrate—passed and repassed like a voluptuous bow. The light movement of their flight never touched the water but caressed our eyes, our hearts, and with each flutter of their tiny wings we fairly swooned. When we saw them returning from the other shore, and quite evidently playing a game and freely disporting themselves over the water, we seemed to hear an exquisite harmony; but taking their time coming back, they made a thousand capricious detours that changed the initial harmonies to an enchantingly fanciful melody. And for our now sonorous souls arose from their silent flight a music of charm and freedom, and all the lovely harmonies of the lake, the woods, the sky, and our own life accompanied them with a magic sweetness that melted us to tears.

I had never spoken to you then and you were, that year, far even from my sight. But how we loved each other in the Engadine! Never could I get enough of you, never once did I let you stay behind me in the house. You accompanied me on all my walks, ate at my table, slept in my bed, dreamed in my soul. One day—is it not possible that some pure instinct, mysterious messenger, apprised you of these childish follies in which you were so intimately involved, in which you shared, yes, actually shared, so literally were you for me a "bodily presence"?—one day (we had neither of us ever been to Italy) we were struck by the word, heard casually spoken, of Alpgrun: "From there you can see as far as Italy." We left for Alpgrun, imagining that the spectacle spreading out beyond the peak where Italy began would have nothing of the real and rough landscape we already knew, and that against a background of dream a totally blue valley would appear. But as we walked along we reminded each other that a frontier does not change the land and that, even if it did, the change would be too gradual for us to notice all at once. Although a little disillusioned, we laughed at ourselves for having been such children.

But, arriving at the summit, we were struck dumb. What we had childishly imagined now, in reality, lay stretched before our eyes. Around us were sparkling glaciers. At our feet torrents ploughed through a wild country of the Engadine, darkly green. Then, a somewhat mysterious hill; and beyond, mauve slopes intermittently revealed and hid a truly blue country—a shining avenue leading into Italy. The names were no longer the same, at once harmonized with this new suavity. The Lake of Poschiavo, the Pizzo de Verone, the Val de Viola, were pointed out to us. After that we went to an extraordinarily wild and solitary place where the desolation of nature and the certainty that here one was completely inaccessible and also invisible, invincible, would have increased the bliss of loving to the point of delirium. I then felt to the full the sadness of not having you with me in your material form, not merely in the garment of my regret but in the reality of my desire. I descended a little lower to the place, still at a great elevation, where tourists come to look at the view. There is a lonely inn there where they write their names. I wrote mine and, beside it, a combination of letters that formed an allusion to yours, for it seemed to me unheard of at the time that I should not leave a proof of your spiritual presence beside me. By putting something of you in the book it seemed to relieve me of some of the obsessive weight with which you oppressed my soul. And besides, I entertained the enormous hope of bringing you there to read the line in the book one day; afterwards you would climb still higher with me to compensate me for all my sadness. Without my saying a word you would understand, or rather you would remember everything; and climbing, you would lean on me with your whole weight as though to make me realize more fully that you were really there; and on your lips, that still kept a trace of the scent of your Egyptian cigarettes, I should find complete oblivion. We would shout aloud the maddest things, reveling in the glorious feeling that not a soul anywhere would hear us; only the short grasses in the little breeze of the heights would shiver. You would be a little out of breath from climbing and have to walk more slowly, while, leaning toward you, I would drink your breath; we would be quite mad. Then, too, we would visit the place where there is a white lake beside a black lake, lovely as a white pearl beside a black pearl. How we would have loved each other in a village lost in the Engadine! We would have allowed no one to come near us but our mountain guides, those immensely tall men whose eyes reflect things so different from those seen in other men's eyes, have a different "water." But now I never think about you any more. Satiety has come without possession. Platonic love also has its saturation point. I have no longer any desire to take you to that country which, without understanding or even knowing it, you bring back to my memory with such touching fidelity. The sight of you has only one charm for me now, that of suddenly recalling those names so full of a strange loveliness, German and Italian: Sils-Maria, Silva Plana, Crestalta, Samaden, Celerina, Juliers, Val de Viola.

 XXIII

Inner Sunset

INTELLIGENCE, like nature, has its spectacles. Neither sunsets nor moonlight, which have how often thrilled me to tears, can ever surpass for me in passionate tenderness that vast melancholy conflagration which, during my walks at the end of the day, colors more mighty floods in my soul than the sun in setting kindles in the sea. Then we hurry our steps in the night. More intoxicated and giddy than a horseman with the ever increasing speed of his adored mount, trembling with joy and confidence, we abandon ourselves to our tumultuous thoughts, and the more we control and direct them the more irresistibly we feel ourselves to be possessed by them. With a tender emotion we wander through the dark countryside and greet the night-dark oaks like the solemn field, like the epic witnesses of the soaring ardor that makes us drunk and sweeps us headlong. Lifting our eyes to the sky, we cannot help feeling an exaltation on recognizing in the openings between the clouds, still aglow with the sun's farewell, the mysterious reflection of our own thoughts; we plunge faster and faster into the darkness and the dog that follows us, the horse that bears us, or the friend who has fallen silent at our side (less perhaps when no other living creature is near us), the flower in our buttonhole, or the cane we twirl joyously with feverish hand, receives from our looks and from our tears the melancholy tribute of our delirium.

 XXIV

As in the Light of the Moon

NIGHT had fallen. I went to my room anxious to be left in darkness, no longer to see the sky and the fields and the sea blazing in the sun. But when I opened my door I found the room illuminated as though by the setting sun. Through the window I could see house, fields, sky and sea; or rather it seemed to me that I "saw them repeated as in a dream"; the gentle moon did not so much reveal them to my eyes as recall them to my memory, flooding them with a pale splendor that failed to dissipate the denser darkness shrouding their forms as by some error. And for hours I remained there looking out of the window at this silent remembrance, vague and pale and spellbound, of things which during the day had given me pleasure or had hurt me with their cries, their voices or their murmurings.

Love is extinct, I stand frightened on the threshold of forgetfulness; but peaceful now and a little pale, here close to me and yet far away and already vague, like the light of the moon, all my joys and all my sorrows, now healed, look at me and are silent. Their silence touches me while their remoteness and their uncertain pallor intoxicate me with sadness and with poetry. And I cannot stop gazing at this moonlight within me.

———————————— XXV ————————————

A Critique of Hope in the Light of Love

HARDLY has the next hour become the present than it is stripped of its charms, finding them again, it is true, if our soul is large enough and well disposed in *perspectives,* when we have left it far behind us on the highroads of memory. Thus the poetic village toward which we hasten the pace of our hopes and of our weary horses, once the hill is passed, again breathes forth those veiled harmonies whose vague promises the vulgarity of its streets, the incongruity of its houses that had melted together into the horizon, the disappearance of the blue mist that had seemed to penetrate it, have failed to keep. But like the alchemist who attributes each one of his failures to an accidental cause and a different one each time, far from suspecting an incurable imperfection in the essence of the present itself, we accuse the malignity of particular circumstances, the exigencies of a certain coveted position, the bad weather or the bad hotels during our trip, of having poisoned our happiness. And, sure of succeeding in eliminating all these destructive causes of our enjoyment, with a sometimes rather reluctant confidence but never disillusioned by a dream come true and therefore disappointing, we continue to count on a dreamed-of future.

But certain thoughtful and moody men who reflect more ardently than others the light of hope, discover quickly enough, alas! that hope does not emanate from the awaited hours but from our own hearts that overflow with rays unknown to nature, pouring them in torrents over hope without rekindling a spark. They have no longer the force to desire what they know is not desirable, to realize dreams which fade as soon as they gather them outside their hearts. This melancholy disposition becomes singularly aggravated and justified in love. Imagination in passing and repassing ceaselessly over its hopes sharpens marvelously its disappointments. Unhappy love, making it impossible for us to know happiness, also prevents our knowing the blanks of boredom. What a lesson in philosophy, what a consolation for old age! For what disappointed ambition can surpass in melancholy the joys of happy love! You love me, my darling; how could you be so cruel as to tell me so? This then is that joy of reciprocated love, the mere thought of which is enough to make me swoon, set my teeth chattering!

I unpin your flowers, I lift your hair, I tear off your jewels, I reach your flesh, my kisses cover, beat on your body like the sea on the sand; but you yourself escape me, and with you happiness. I must leave you, I go home alone and sad. Blaming this final calamity, I return to you forever; my last illusion has been torn away, I am forever unhappy.

I don't know how I had the courage to tell you this; it is the happiness of my entire life that I have pitilessly cast away, or at least the consolation, for your eyes, whose happy confidence still intoxicated me at times, will now reflect nothing but painful disenchantment, of which your wisdom and your disappointments had already warned you. Since this secret, which one of us had been hiding from the other, has now been spoken aloud, there is no happiness possible for us any longer. Not even the disinterested joys of hope are left us. Hope is an act of faith. Its credulity has been undeceived. It is dead. Not expecting any further enjoyment, we cannot now bewitch ourselves with hope. To hope without hope, which would be the wise thing to do, is impossible.

But come nearer to me, my dear little friend. Dry your eyes and look—I don't know whether it is my tears that blur my sight, but it seems to me I can make out, over there behind us, great bonfires being lighted. Oh! my dear, how I love you! Give me your hand and let us go, but without getting too close to those beautiful flames. . . . I think it must be that indulgent and powerful Memory wishes us well, and that she is about to do a great deal for us, my dear.

XXVI

Forest Scene

WE HAVE nothing to fear and a great deal to learn from trees, that vigorous and pacific tribe which without stint produces strengthening essences for us, soothing balms, and in whose gracious company we spend so many cool, silent and intimate hours. On those scorching afternoons when, by its very excess, the light is invisible to our eyes, let us go down into one of those Norman "bottoms" out of which lithely spring tall, thick beeches whose foliage holds back, like a thin but resistant shore, that ocean of light, keeping only a few drops that tinkle melodiously in the black silence under the trees. Here our mind enjoys, not as by the sea, on the plains, or in the mountains, the pleasure of spreading out over the world, but the happiness of being separated from it; and hemmed in on all sides by the ineradicably rooted trunks, it leaps upward after the manner of the trees. Lying on our back, our head resting on the dry leaves, from the bosom of profound repose we can follow the joyous agility of our mind mounting, without making one leaf tremble, to the highest branches, where it perches on the edge of the lovely sky beside a singing bird. Here and there a little sunlight lies stagnant at the foot of the trees, in which, at times, it dips and gilds the leaves of its lowest branches. Everything else, relaxed and stationary, is silent in a dusky happiness. Soaring and erect within the vast offering of their branches, and yet peaceful and calm, the trees' strange and natural pose invites us with gracious murmurings to join in this life, so ancient and so young, so different from our own, of which it seems to be the mysterious reverse.

A light breeze for a moment disturbs their shining and somber immobility, and they tremble a little, balancing the sunlight on their crests and stirring the shadows at their feet.

Petit-Abbeville (Dieppe), August, 1895

XXVII

Horse-Chestnut Trees

I USED to love to pause under the enormous horse-chestnut trees, particularly after autumn had yellowed their leaves. How many hours have I spent in those mysterious greenish grottos, looking overhead at the murmuring cascades of pale gold that poured coolness and twilight over me! I envied the robins and the squirrels living in those frail and profound pavilions of verdure among the branches, those ancient hanging-gardens that every new spring, for two hundred years, has covered with white and fragrant blossoms. The branches, imperceptibly curved, swept nobly down from the tree toward the ground, as though they were other trees that had been planted in the trunk head first. The pallor of the remaining leaves made the branches stand out and seem more solid and blacker from being stripped, and thus attached to the trunk, they looked like a magnificent comb restraining the trees' spreading golden tresses.

Reveillon, October, 1895

XXVIII

The Sea

THE SEA will always fascinate those who have known the disgust of life and the lure of mystery even before their first sorrows, like a presentiment of the inadequacy of reality to satisfy them. Those who feel the need of rest, even before they have experienced fatigue, the sea will console and vaguely exhilarate. Unlike the earth, it bears no traces of men's toil and of their lives. There, nothing remains, nothing passes save in flight, and how quickly vanish the tracks of the ships sailing over it. Hence that perfect purity of the sea unknown to the things of the earth. And this virgin water is much more delicate than the hardened earth, which it takes a pick to dent. A child's footstep, with a tinkling sound, will cut a deep furrow in the water and for a moment the blending shades are broken up; then all trace is obliterated and the sea becomes calm again as in the first days of creation. The man who is weary of the paths of the earth or who divines, even before he has tried them, how bitter and vulgar they are, will be enchanted by the pale highroads of the sea, more dangerous and lovelier, more dubious and lonelier. There everything is more mysterious, even those great cloud shadows that sometimes float peacefully over the bare fields of the sea without houses and without shade—those celestial hamlets, those unsubstantial tenuous boughs.

The sea has the charm of things that do not fall silent at night, that, in the midst of our unquiet lives, give us the right to sleep, the assurance that everything will not be annihilated, like the night-light which makes little children feel less alone when it is shining. It is not separated from the sky like the earth, is always in harmony with the sky's colors, is affected by its most delicate shadings. It beams in the sunlight and every evening seems to die at the same hour. And after the sun has disappeared the sea seems to pine for it still and to preserve its luminous remembrance in the face of the uniformly somber earth. It is at this moment when it glows with such melancholy and sweet reflections that, contemplating it, our hearts melt. When night has almost fallen, when the sky is dark over a blackened earth, it goes on gleaming faintly, who knows by what unknown miracle, by what bright remnant of the day buried beneath its waves?

It refreshes our imagination because it does not remind us of the life of men, but it rejoices the soul because like the soul it is infinite and ineffectual aspiration, striving, forever broken by a fall, eternal and sweet lamentation. It enchants us like music, which, unlike language, bears no trace of material things, which never speaks to us of men, but imitates the movements of our soul. Our heart leaps up with its waves, falls back with them, forgetting thus its own falterings, and consoles itself in a secret harmony between its own sadness and that of the sea, which confounds its destiny with that of all things.

September, 1892

——————————— XXIX ———————————

A Marine

PERHAPS those words whose meaning I have lost will have to be explained to me again by all the things which for so long have known the path by which to reach me, and, although for many years abandoned, it could, I truly believe, be used again, is not forever closed. It would be necessary to return to Normandy, not force myself, stay quietly by the sea. Or rather I should have to take the wooded paths from which it can be glimpsed from time to time, and where the breeze mingles the odor of salt, wet leaves and milk. I should ask nothing of all these natal things. They are generous to the child they have known since birth, and would of themselves bring back to him all those forgotten things. Everything, and first of all the smell of it, would herald the presence of the sea. I should not have seen it yet, but only faintly heard it. Following the hawthorn path I used to know so well, I should be filled with tenderness, and dismay too at suddenly catching sight of it through an opening in the hedge—that invisible and present friend, that wayward, ever complaining woman, that melancholy old queen, the sea. Then suddenly it would appear. It would be on one of those somnolent days of bright sun when the sea reflects the sky, blue like itself, but paler. White sails like butterflies would be resting on the motionless water, no longer wanting to stir, as though swooning in the heat. Or, on the contrary, it would be agitated, yellowish under the sun like a field of mud, with great swelling waves that from a distance would seem to be stationary, crowned with dazzling snow.

XXX

Harbor Sails

IN THE harbor, narrow and long like a street made of water between low wharves twinkling with the evening lights, the passers-by stopped to look at the ships assembled there like noble strangers arrived the day before and ready to leave again. Indifferent to the curiosity they excited in the crowd and seeming to scorn its lowliness, or simply unable to speak its language, they still retained, in their watery inn where they had stopped for the night, their silent and motionless *élan.* The sturdiness of their stems spoke no less of long voyages still ahead than their visible damages of hardships already endured on those slippery highroads, ancient as the world and new as the passage of the ship that furrows them, and which they will not survive. Frail and resistant, they were turned with haughty sadness toward the Ocean over which they towered, and where they seemed as though lost. The marvelous and cunning complexity of the rigging was reflected in the water like a wise and wary intelligence that dives into an uncertain future which sooner or later will destroy it. So recently withdrawn from the terrible and beautiful life into which they will plunge again tomorrow, their sails were still listless from the wind which had swelled them, their bowsprits were poised obliquely over the water as they themselves had been yesterday in their flight, and from stem to stern the curve of their hull seemed to have kept the same mysterious and sinuous grace of their watery tracks.

The Melancholy Summer
of
Madame de Breyves

"Ariadne, O my Sister, by what a love wounded
Have you died, on those same shores abandoned!"

—————————— I ——————————

FRANÇOISE DE BREYVES that evening could not
make up her mind whether to go to the reception
of the Princess Elizabeth A . . ., to the opera, or
to see the Livrays' plays.

At the house where she had dined, they had left the
table more than an hour ago. She really must decide.

Her friend Genevieve, who was to leave with her,
wanted to go to the reception, while Madame de Breyves would have preferred either of the other alternatives, or even a third, going home to bed. The carriage
was announced. She was still undecided.

"Really," said Genevieve, "you're being horrid—
Reske is probably going to sing and that would amuse
me. One would think something dreadful was going

to happen to you if you went to Elizabeth's. Besides, you know, you haven't been to one of her big affairs this season, and being such a close friend it's really not nice of you."

Françoise, since the death of her husband, who had left her a widow at twenty—that was four years ago— rarely went anywhere without Genevieve and always tried to please her. She could resist no longer, and after taking leave of her hosts and of the guests, disappointed at the departure of one of the most popular women of Paris, said to the footman, "To the Princess A . . .'s."

II

THE EVENING at the Princess A . . .'s was very boring. Once Madame de Breyves asked Genevieve, "Who is the young man who escorted you to the buffet?"

"He is a M. de Laléande whom I never heard of. Would you like me to introduce him? In fact, he asked me to, but I was evasive because he is so insignificant and boring, and as he thinks you very pretty, you'd never get rid of him."

"Then decidedly no!" said Françoise. "Besides, he's rather ugly and vulgar-looking in spite of his beautiful eyes."

"You are right," said Genevieve. "And as you would be meeting him often it might be embarrassing if you knew him."

Then she added, laughing, "Unless, of course, you'd

like a more intimate acquaintance—in that case you're missing a fine opportunity."

"Yes, a fine opportunity," said Françoise, already thinking of something else.

"But after all," Genevieve added, probably seized with remorse at having been such an unfaithful emissary, gratuitously depriving the young man of a pleasure, "this is one of the last affairs of the season, so it wouldn't really matter and might be more civil."

"So be it, if he comes over this way."

He was on the other side of the drawing-room facing them, and did not come over.

"We should be going," Genevieve said a moment later.

"Oh, just a second," said Françoise.

And out of caprice, above all impelled by an urge to flirt with a young man who must indeed find her pretty, she began to look at him a little lingeringly, quickly dropping her eyes, and then staring at him again. She made her expression as caressing as possible, she hardly knew why, for no reason, for the pleasure of it, the pleasure of being charitable, the pleasure of vanity too and of futility, the pleasure of those who write their names on trees for a passer-by they will never see, of those who throw bottles into the ocean. It was getting late. M. de Laléande was going toward the door. As it remained open after he had left, Madame de Breyves could see him at the other end of the entrance-hall holding out his number to the cloak-room attendant.

"You're right. We really must be going," she said to Genevieve.

They both rose. But by chance Genevieve being detained by one of her friends for a moment, Françoise was left alone near the cloak-room. There was no one there at the moment but M. de Laléande, who could not find his cane. To amuse herself, Françoise gave him one last lingering look. He passed close to her, lightly rubbing his elbow against hers, and while still touching her, his eyes very bright, and still pretending to be looking for his cane, said, "Come to my place, 5 Rue Royale."

This was something she had so little anticipated, and M. de Laléande was so seriously searching for his cane again, that she was never able to decide later whether it was only an hallucination or not. Above all she was horribly frightened and, Prince A . . . passing just then, she called to him and began talking volubly, arranging for an outing the next day. During this conversation M. de Laléande had left. In another moment Genevieve arrived and the two women took their departure. Madame de Breyves said nothing. She was still shocked and flattered and, at bottom, indifferent. Two days later, recalling the incident by chance, she began to wonder if M. de Laléande had really spoken those words. Trying in vain to remember, she decided she must have heard them as in a dream, and that the movement of his elbow had been involuntary. Then she thought no more of M. de Laléande and when by chance she heard his name mentioned, she vaguely recalled his face but had entirely forgotten what must have been an hallucination outside the cloak-room.

She saw him again at the last reception of the season (June was nearly over), dared not ask to have him presented and yet, in spite of the fact that she thought him almost ugly, knew he was not intelligent, felt a desire to meet him. She went up to Genevieve and said, "After all, you might introduce M. de Laléande. I don't like to be impolite. But don't say I suggested it, for I don't want to get myself involved."

"All right, later if we see him. He isn't around just now."

"But can't you look for him?"

"He may have left."

"Oh, no," Françoise said quickly, "he couldn't have left, it's too early. Oh, twelve o'clock already! Darling, please, it isn't so difficult. The other evening you were keen on it. It has a special interest for me."

Genevieve looked at her, a little surprised, and went in search of M. de Laléande. He had left.

"You see I was right," said Genevieve, coming back to Françoise.

"I'm too bored for words," said Françoise, "and I have a headache. Let's go home. Do you mind?"

III

FRANÇOISE never missed an evening at the Opera now and, with vague hope, accepted all the dinner invitations she received. Two weeks went by without her seeing M. de Laléande again, and she would wake up in the night trying to devise some scheme for meeting him. While all the time repeating to herself that he was boring and not even handsome, she thought of him more than of all the witty and charming men she knew. The season being over, there would be no chance of seeing him again, and she decided to create an opportunity, thought of nothing else.

One evening she said to Genevieve, "Didn't you tell me that you knew a M. de Laléande?"

"Jacques de Laléande? Yes and no; he was introduced to me, but he never left cards and I don't see him."

"Well, you know, I have a certain interest, a considerable interest, I might say—oh, nothing to do with me, and I can't say anything about it for a month" (before then she would have devised with him some plausible story, and the thought of a secret shared with him alone gave her a delicious thrill) "in seeing and talking to him. Do try to manage it, because now that the season is over there won't be any more parties where I might meet him."

The practice of close friendship, so purifying when it is sincere, saved Genevieve, as well as Françoise, from that curiosity which is the shameful amusement of most people in society. So it was that Genevieve with all her heart and without for an instant entertaining the intention or the desire or even an idea of questioning her friend, began her search for M. de

Laléande, distressed only because she was unable to find him.

"It is unfortunate that Elizabeth A . . . has left. Of course there is M. de Grumello, but that doesn't help us very much, for what are we to say to him? Oh! I have an idea. M. de Laléande plays the cello—badly, but that doesn't matter. M. de Grumello admires him and is so stupid and besides, he would be overjoyed to please you. The only thing is—you've always avoided him and, as you hate dropping people after making use of them, you would be obliged to invite him next season."

But Françoise was already flushed with joy. "That doesn't matter, I don't care; I'd invite all the upstarts and adventurers of Paris if necessary. Oh! please, darling, don't waste a second!"

And Genevieve wrote:

"*Monsieur,*

"You know that I would do anything in the world to please my friend, Madame de Breyves, whom you must have met. I have heard her say several times, when the cello was mentioned, how much she regretted never having heard your good friend M. de Laléande play. I wonder if you could get him to play for her and for me. Now that we all have more time, perhaps this will not inconvenience you too much, and it would be very good of you. With kindest regards,

"Alériouvre Buivres"

"Take this letter to M. de Grumello," Françoise

said to a servant. "Do not wait for an answer, but make sure that he receives it at once."

The next day Genevieve had M. de Grumello's reply taken by hand to Madame de Breyves:

"Madame,

"I should have been more delighted than you can imagine to have been able to satisfy your desire and that of Madame de Breyves, whom I know slightly but for whom I feel the most respectful and the keenest sympathy. And I am utterly disconsolate that by a most unhappy chance M. de Laléande left for Biarritz two days ago, where, alas! he will remain for several months.

"Please accept, Madame, etc.

"Grumello"

Françoise, as white as a sheet, rushed to her room to lock herself in. She had hardly time to reach it before she was shaken by sobs and tears were flowing. Until then, preoccupied as she had been in imagining all sorts of romantic ways of meeting and knowing him, believing that she could realize them when she wished, she had been, perhaps unconsciously, living on this desire and this hope. Deeply implanted in her, they had sent down a thousand little imperceptible roots and started a new mysterious sap coursing through her. And now, all at once, they were uprooted and thrown into the discard. She suffered the agonizing laceration of that hidden self suddenly torn up by the roots. Now she saw clearly through all the lies that hope and desire had held out to her, and, at last, from the depths of her grief came suddenly face to face with the reality of her love.

—————————— IV ——————————

EVERY DAY Françoise seemed to grow more and more indifferent to all her habitual pleasures. Even from her most intense and intimate joys, those shared with her mother and with Genevieve, even from the hours she gave to music, from her reading, from her walks, her heart was absent, devoured by a jealous sorrow that never left her. And she felt that there was no end to this pain, since it was impossible for her to go to Biarritz and, even had that been possible, she was determined not to compromise by any desperate action the prestige she might enjoy in the eyes of M. de Laléande. Poor little victim, tortured without knowing why, she was terrified to think that this suffering might last for months without relief, drive away sleep, trouble her dreams. She worried, too, thinking that, without her knowing it, he might pass through Paris again. And her fear of letting happiness so near at hand once more escape her gave her the courage to send a servant to make inquiries of M. de Laléande's concierge. He knew nothing. Then, realizing that there was now no hope of a sail appearing on the horizon of this sea of sorrow which spread out infinitely, and beyond which it seemed there was nothing, and that earth had ended, she felt she was being driven to some folly, what, she did not know—writing to him, perhaps—and to calm herself a little, becoming her own doctor, she decided on a scheme for letting him know that she had deliberately tried to see him. To that end she wrote to M. de Grumello:

"*Monsieur,*

"Madame de Buivres has told me of your kind thought. How touched I was, how grateful to you! But there is something that worries me. Did M. de Laléande think me indiscreet? In case you do not know, would you ask him, and when you have found out let me know, and promise to tell me the exact truth. I am curious, and you would be doing me a kindness. Again thank you, *Monsieur,* etc.

"Voragines Breyves"

One hour later a servant brought this letter:

"You have no cause to worry, Madame, M. de Laléande does not know of your request to hear him play. I wrote asking him what days he would be free to play at my house without mentioning for whom. He replied from Biarritz that he would not be in Paris again till January. You must not thank me. My greatest joy would be to add the merest trifle to yours, etc."

"Grumello"

There was nothing more she could do. She gave up trying and grew sadder and sadder, saddening her mother, ashamed of her sadness. She went to spend a few days in the country, then left for Trouville. She heard people discussing M. de Laléande's social ambitions, and when a prince, trying his best to be agreeable to her, said: "What can I do that would please you most?" she felt almost like laughing when she thought of his surprise if she were to answer truthfully, and felt all the concentrated and bitter irony of the contrast between the great and difficult things always being done for her, and the one little thing, so easy and so impossible, that would have brought back peace, health and happiness to her, and the happiness of those dearest to her. She only knew a little relief when she was alone with the servants who waited on her, sensing her sadness. Their respectful and grieved silence spoke to her of M. de Laléande. It gave her a voluptuous pleasure, and she would make them serve her luncheon slowly, lingering over it, to put off the moment when she would have to see her friends and to dissimulate her sorrow. She wanted to relish the sweet and bitter taste of the sadness that, because of him, surrounded her. She would have liked to see more people dominated by him, to feel that what took up so much room in her heart was also occupying a little of the space around her. She would have liked to possess healthy, lively animals who, gradually stricken with her ill, would go into a decline. Desperate at moments, she wanted to write to him, have someone write, demean herself. "Nothing mattered any longer." But she was restrained by the thought that even in the interest of her love she must keep her position in society, since it might give her greater power over him one day, if that day ever came. And if a short intimacy with him should break the spell he had cast over her (she did not wish to believe, could not believe, or even imagine it, for an instant, but her mind, more discerning than her blind heart, foresaw the cruel eventuality), she would be left without a single support in the world. And if some other love should come to her, she would lack all the resources of this power which on her return to Paris would facilitate her intimacy with M. de Laléande. Trying to separate her feelings from herself and to examine them as an object, she would say to herself: "I know that he is mediocre and have always known it. That was my first opinion of him. It has not changed. Since then emotion has intervened but without, for all that, altering my opinion. He is nothing at all and it is for this nonentity I live. I live for Jacques de Laléande." But as soon as she had said his name, by an involuntary association, this time unanalyzed, she could see him again, and felt such contentment and such pain that she knew that it did not matter what a nonentity he really was, since he gave her the sensation of joys and sorrows compared to which others were as nothing. And although she realized that when she came to know him better all this would disappear, this mirage still constituted all the reality of her pain and voluptuous pleasure. A phrase from *Die Meistersinger* she had heard that evening at the Princess A . . .'s had the power of bringing him vividly back to her (*Dem Vogel der heut sang dem war der Schnabel hold gewach-*

sen). Unconsciously it had become for her the *leit-
motif* of M. de Laléande, and, hearing it one day at
a concert in Trouville, she had burst into tears. From
time to time, not too often, for fear of mitigating the
effect, she would lock herself in her room and, sitting
at the piano (she had had it brought for no other
purpose), would begin to play, closing her eyes to see
him the more clearly. It was her sole intoxicating joy
that ended in disillusionment, the opium she craved.
Sometimes stopping to listen to the flow of her sorrow,
as one leans over a spring to hear the sweet and cease-
less lamentation of the water, and thinking of the
atrocious alternatives before her: either future shame
and the despair of those dear to her, or (if she did not
yield) her own eternal sorrow—she would revile herself for having so artfully measured the doses of pleasure and pain of her love, which she had been powerless to reject at once as an invidious poison, or later to
cure. Above all she reviled her eyes, or perhaps even
before them her sense of curiosity and of coquetry
which had made them open like flowers to tempt the
young man, and had then exposed her to M. de Laléande's own glances as sure as arrows and more invinc-
ibly sweet than shots of morphine. She reviled her
imagination too. So tenderly had she nurtured it that
she sometimes wondered if it alone had not given
birth to this love which now tyrannized over its
mother and tortured her. She reviled her ingenuity
which had so cleverly, so well and so ill, contrived so
many romances for their meeting that their hopeless

impossibility had perhaps bound her even more irrevocably to their hero; reviled the uprightness and the
delicacy of her heart which would, if she should give
herself, poison with remorse and shame all the joys of
her guilty love; reviled her will, so impetuous, so
headstrong, so bold in leaping over obstacles when
her desires drove her toward an impossible goal, so
weak, so soft, so broken, not only when they had to be
denied, but when some other emotion seized and carried her away. Finally she reviled her mind in its di-
vinest form, that supreme gift she had received, and
which is given every imaginable name without the
true one ever being found—poet's intuition, ecstasy of
the believer, profound sense of nature and of music—
which had set up before her love infinite heights and
horizons, had let it bathe in the supernatural light
of her love's own charm and had, in return, lent to
her love something of itself, had interested in this
love, associated and confounded with it all its deepest
and most secret inner life, had consecrated to it, like
the treasures of the church to the Madonna, all the
most precious gems of her imagination and her heart,
which, in the evening or on the water, she would hear
lamenting, whose melancholy and her own, at never
seeing him now, were sisters; she reviled that inexpressible feeling of the mystery of things, when our
spirit loses itself in the radiance of beauty like that of
the sun when it sinks into the sea, for having deep-
ened her love, for having immaterialized, broadened,
infinitized it without, for all that, making it less ago-

nizing, for as Baudelaire says (speaking of the end of autumn days), "there are certain delicious sensations which are no less intense for being vague; and there is no sharper point than that of infinity."

——————————— V ———————————

"... and was consumed from the rising of the Sun on the seaweed by the shore, keeping in the depths of his heart like an arrow in the liver, the burning wound of the great Kypris."

—THEOCRITUS: *The Cyclops*

I HAVE JUST come across Madame de Breyves again here at Trouville. I have known her in happier hours. Nothing can cure her. If only she loved M. de Laléande because he was handsome or because he was witty, one could hope to find a handsomer and a wittier young man to distract her. If it were his kindness or his love for her that had attracted her, someone else might try loving her with greater fidelity. But M. de Laléande is neither handsome nor intelligent, has had no opportunity of proving whether he is tender or brutal, fickle or faithful. It is then really himself she loves, not his merits nor his charms, which can be found to as high a degree in others; it is really himself she loves in spite of his imperfections, in spite of his mediocrity; therefore, in spite of everything, she is doomed to love him. *Himself*, does she know what that is? except that it is something that has caused her such shudders of desolation or felicity that the rest of

her life has counted for nothing, nothing else has mattered. The most beautiful physiognomy, the most
original intelligence would not have that particular
and mysterious essence, so unique that no human being will ever find his exact double in all the infinitude
of worlds, in the whole eternity of time. If it hadn't
been for Genevieve de Buivres, who innocently insisted on her going to Madame A . . .'s, all this would
not have happened. Caught by circumstances and imprisoned, she is the victim of an ill for which there is
no remedy because it is without a reason. Certainly
M. de Laléande, who is probably leading a very banal
life on the beach at Biarritz, indulging in harmless
dreams, would be very much astonished if he knew of
this other existence of his, so miraculously intense that
it subordinates everything to itself, annihilates everything that is not itself, if he knew that in Madame de
Breyves' soul he enjoyed an existence as continuous as
his own personal existence, manifested just as effectively in actions, differing only in its heightened consciousness, less intermittent, more abundant. How
surprised he would be if he knew that he, ordinarily
so little sought after in his fleshly guise, is an object
of interest wherever Madame de Breyves goes, among
the most highly gifted people, in the most exclusive
drawing-rooms, amidst scenery quite sufficient in itself, and that this woman, so popular everywhere, has
not a thought, not a feeling, not an attention for anything but the recollection of this intruder before
whom everything else fades, as though he alone were

a real person and the persons present as vain as memories or shadows.

Whether Madame de Breyves takes a walk with a poet or lunches with an archduchess, whether she is alone and reading or talking with a cherished friend, whether she rides horseback or sleeps, the name, the image of M. de Laléande is always over her, deliciously, cruelly, inevitably as the sky is over our heads. She has even reached the point, she who always detested Biarritz, where she finds in everything connected with that city a touching and painful charm. She is preoccupied with the people who are there, or those who are about to go and who will see him, perhaps, without knowing it, who will live with him without joy. She bears them no grudge and, without daring to give them any messages, questions them ceaselessly, wondering sometimes how, hearing her talk continually about all the things surrounding her secret, no one has guessed it. A huge photograph of Biarritz is one of the only ornaments in her room. She imagines that one of the strollers in it looks like M. de Laléande. If she knew the cheap music he liked, those despised songs would without a doubt soon take the place, on her piano and in her heart, of the symphonies of Beethoven and the operas of Wagner, both because they have lowered her standards and because of the charm that he, from whom all charm and all sorrow now come, casts over them. Sometimes the image of this man whom she has seen twice only, and then only for an instant, who occupies such a tiny place in the exterior events of her life but in her heart and in her mind one so exorbitant that it absorbs them altogether, grows blurred before the tired eyes of her memory. She no longer sees him, cannot remember his features, his form, has almost forgotten even his eyes. Yet this image is all she has of him. She is beside herself at the thought that she might lose it, that her desire—which it is true tortures her but which is now her whole self, in which she has taken refuge after fleeing all the rest, to which she clings as one clings to one's own conservation, one's life, good or bad—might vanish and that he would leave her with nothing but the uneasiness and desolation of a dream, no longer knowing the object that has caused them, would no longer see him even in her mind in which she could no longer cherish him. Then suddenly, after the momentary blurring of her inner vision, his image returns. Her sorrow can begin again, and it is now almost a joy.

How will Madame de Breyves endure her return to Paris, from which, until January, he will still be absent? What will she do from now until then? What will she do—what will he do—afterwards?

A dozen times I have been on the point of going to Biarritz to bring back M. de Laléande. The consequences might well be terrible, but speculation is futile, since she will not hear of it. But I am desolate, seeing her little temples beaten from within, seeing her shattered by the blows without surcease of this inexplicable passion. Her whole life follows its rhythm in an anguished mode. Often she imagines that he will come to Trouville, come up to her, tell her that he loves her. She sees him; his eyes shine. He speaks to her in that colorless voice of dream which prevents our believing, while all the time forcing us to listen. It is he. He speaks the words that intoxicate even though we hear them only in dreams, when we see, radiant and touching, the divine and confident smile of two destinies uniting. And then almost at once she is awakened by the feeling that the two worlds, the world of reality and the world of her desire, are parallel, that it is as impossible for them ever to meet as a shadow the body that projected it. Then, remembering that moment by the cloak-room when her elbow rubbed his elbow, when he offered her that body which, if she had wished, if she had known, she might now be clasping to her own, and which is now far away, perhaps forever, she feels cries of despair and revolt rising in her from all sides, like those one hears on sinking ships. If sometimes, walking along the beach or in the woods, she lets the pleasure of contemplation or of reverie, or even a sweet odor, or a song brought from a distance and muffled by the breeze, gently take possession of her, make her for an instant forget her pain, all at once she feels a terrible blow and a wound in her heart—and above the waves, higher than the leaves, in the misty horizon of woods or sea, she catches sight of the vague image of her invisible and ever-present conqueror, his eyes shining through the clouds, as on the day when he offered himself to her, and sees him vanish with the quiver from which he has taken and let fly another arrow.

July, 1893

The End of Jealousy

"Whether we ask for them or not, give us good things, and
keep evils from us even though we ask them of thee.
"This prayer seems fine and sure. If you find anything in it
to take issue with do not conceal it."

—PLATO

My LITTLE TREE, my little donkey, my mother,
my brother, my country, my little God, my little
sea-shell, my lotus flower, my little stranger, my darling, my little plant, do go away and let me dress, and
I'll meet you, Rue de la Baume, at eight o'clock. But
please don't be any later than quarter past, because
I am very hungry."

She tried to close the door on Honoré, but again
he said, "Neck!" and at once she held out her neck to
him with a docility and exorbitant alacrity that made
him burst out laughing.

"Even if you objected," he said, "there would still
exist between your neck and my mouth, between your
ears and my mustache, between your hands and my
hands, little personal understandings. I am sure they
would go on even if we stopped loving each other,

just as my valet, since my quarrel with my cousin Pauline, for all I can do, continues to go to see her maid every evening. It is entirely of itself, without my consent, that my mouth goes toward your neck."

They were now a step apart. Suddenly their eyes met and each one tried to fix in the eyes of the other the idea of their love; for a second she remained standing thus, then fell panting into a chair as though she had been running. And they said almost at the same instant, with a grave exaltation, pronouncing emphatically, their lips formed as for a kiss, "My love!"

With a little shake of her head she repeated in a sad and doleful tone, "Yes, my love. . . ."

She knew that he could not resist that little movement of her head. He threw himself on her, kissing her, and then said very slowly, "Cruel!" and so tenderly that her eyes filled with tears.

Half past seven struck. He left.

Returning home, Honoré kept repeating to himself, "My mother, my brother, my country—" He stopped. "Yes, my country! . . . my little tree, my little seashell." And he couldn't help laughing as he said these words which they had so quickly adopted as their own, seemingly so empty but that for them were filled with infinite meaning. Giving themselves up without thinking to the inventive and fertile genius of their love, it had, little by little, provided them with a language, as nations are provided with arms, games and laws.

While dressing for dinner his thoughts were un-

consciously hanging on the moment when he would
see her again, just as an acrobat already touches the
distant trapeze as he flies toward it, or as a musical
phrase seems to reach the chord that will resolve it,
drawing it across the distance separating them by the
very force of the desire that presages and summons it.
And it was in this way that Honoré had soared
through life during the past year, from the minute he
awoke hurrying toward the hour when he would see
her, and his days were not in reality composed of
twelve or fourteen hours, but of four or five half-
hours and of their anticipation and of their remembrance.

Honoré had been at the Princess d'Alériouvre's several minutes when Madame Seaune arrived. She
greeted her hostess and a few of the guests, but when
she held out her hand to Honoré she seemed not so
much to greet him as to be taking his hand as she
might have done in the middle of a conversation. If
their liaison had been known, people might have
thought they had come together and that to avoid
entering the room at the same time she had waited a
moment outside the door. But even if they had not
seen each other for two days (which for a year had not
yet happened) they would still not have felt that joyous surprise at meeting which is at the bottom of all
friendly greetings, for, not being able to remain five
minutes without thinking of each other, they could
never meet, never having left each other.

During dinner, whenever they spoke to each other, their manner in eagerness and affectionate tenderness went beyond that of simple friends, and was impregnated with a majestic and natural respect unknown to lovers. Thus they appeared like the gods who, as fable has it, lived in disguise among men, or like two angels whose fraternal intimacy, while exalting their joy, in no way lessens the respect that the nobility of their common origin and their mysterious blood inspire. While the air was redolent with the potency of the irises and roses that reigned languidly over the table, little by little, it was filled as well with the perfume of that tenderness, as naturally exhaled. At certain moments it seemed to perfume the room with a violence that nature would not allow them to moderate any more than it allows the heliotrope to moderate its perfume in the sun, or in the rain the flowering lilacs.

So it was that their tenderness, for not being secret, was all the more mysterious. It was there for all to observe, like those enigmatic and defenseless bracelets on the arm of a woman in love, on which are inscribed in unknown but visible characters the name that for her means life and death, seeming to be offering their meaning to curious and disappointed eyes that fail to grasp it.

"How much longer am I going to love her?" Honoré asked himself as he rose from the table. He remembered how brief had been his other passions which at the beginning had seemed immortal, and the certainty that this one would some day come to an end saddened his feeling of tenderness.

Then he remembered the priest that morning at mass reading from the Gospels: "Jesus stretched forth His hand and said to them: This is my mother and my sister and all my brethren." Trembling, he had for an instant lifted up his whole soul to God, but very high like a palm tree, and had prayed: "My God! My God! grant me by Thy grace that I shall love her forever. My God, this grace alone I ask, my God, Thou who hast the power, grant that I shall love her forever!"

Now in one of those purely physical moments when the soul within us hides behind the digesting stomach, behind the skin that still enjoys the recent shower and the sensation of fine linen, the mouth that smokes, the eye that takes delight in bare shoulders and bright lights, he repeated his prayer with less conviction, no longer really believing in the miracle that would reverse the psychological law of his inconstancy, just as difficult to circumvent as the physical laws of gravitation or of death.

She noticed his preoccupied expression, got up and came over to him without his seeing her, and as they were some distance from the others, in that drawling, forlorn tone, that little-girl tone which always made him laugh, and as though he had spoken to her, said, "What?"

He laughed. "If you say another word I'll kiss you, I swear I will, in front of everybody!"

She laughed too at first, then to amuse him, assuming her sad little pouting air again, said, "So that's it! You weren't thinking of me at all!"

And he, looking at her and still laughing, replied, "Little liar!" and added softly, "Naughty! Naughty!"

She left him to join the others. Honoré thought: "I shall try, when I feel my heart leaving her, to withdraw it so softly she will not even guess. I shall always be just as tender, just as respectful. I shall hide from her the new love that will have replaced my love for her, as carefully as today I hide those pleasures that only my body enjoys away from her." (He glanced over at the Princess d'Alériouvre.) And as for her, he would let her center her life, little by little, elsewhere by means of other attachments. He would not be jealous, would himself suggest the men who would seem to him the most capable of offering her a more decent or more glorious homage. The more he thought of Françoise as a woman he no longer loved, but whose spiritual charms he would continue to relish to the full, the more sharing her seemed to him simple and noble. Gentle and tolerant words of friendship, of splendid generosity to be displayed toward those worthy of the best one has, rose readily to his lips.

At that instant Françoise, seeing that it was ten o'clock, said good night and left. Honoré escorted her to her carriage, imprudently kissed her under cover of the night, and returned.

Three hours later, Honoré was walking home accompanied by M. de Buivres, whose return from Tonkin they had been celebrating. Honoré questioned him about the Princess d'Alériouvre, who, left a widow at about the same time, was far more beautiful than Françoise. Without being in love with her, Honoré would have enjoyed possessing her, if he could have been sure that Françoise would not find out, not be made unhappy. "No one seems to know anything about her," said M. de Buivres, "or, at least, not when I left, for I have seen no one since my return."

"In short, no prospects there tonight," concluded Honoré.

"No, not much," replied M. de Buivres, and as they had reached Honoré's door the conversation came to an end. Then M. de Buivres added, "Except Madame Seaune, whom you must have met, since you were there for dinner too. If she strikes your fancy—it's simple. For my part, I can't see her in that light."

"But I never heard anything like that before," said Honoré.

"You're young," replied M. de Buivres. "Come to think of it, there was someone there tonight who had quite an affair with her. I'm pretty sure it was that young François de Gouvres. He says she is passionate! But rather an ugly body. He didn't care about going on. I'll wager that she's enjoying herself at this very moment. Have you noticed how she always leaves any affair early?"

"But she lives in the same house with her brother

since her husband's death—surely she wouldn't risk
having the concierge tell her brother that she came in
at all hours."

"But between ten o'clock and one o'clock in the
morning, my boy, there's time for a lot of things!
Who knows? But it's nearly one now. I must let you
get to bed."

He rang the bell for Honoré; in an instant the door
was opened; and as he held out his hand, Honoré
said good night mechanically and entered. He immediately felt a wild desire to go out again, but the door
had closed heavily behind him, and except for his
candle waiting for him patiently at the foot of the
stairs, the place was in darkness. He did not dare wake
the concierge again to open the door for him, and
went upstairs to his apartment.

II

"Our acts our angels are, or good or ill,
Our fatal shadows that walk by us still."
—JOHN FLETCHER

LIFE had indeed changed for Honoré since the day
when M. de Buivres had made, among so many others,
remarks—no different from those Honoré himself had
listened to or uttered so many times with complete
indifference—but that he now kept hearing during
the day whenever he was alone, and all night long.
He had immediately questioned Françoise, who loved
him much too dearly and felt his grief too keenly to

think of taking offense. She swore she had never deceived him and that she would never deceive him.

When he was with her, when he held her little hands, murmuring Verlaine's line to them,

Belles petites mains qui fermerez mes yeux,

when he heard her say, "My brother, my country, my beloved," and when her voice echoed lingeringly in his heart with the sweetness of childhood bells, he believed her. And if he did not feel so happy as before, at least it no longer seemed impossible to him that his convalescent heart would one day find happiness again. But when he was away from Françoise, sometimes even when, being with her, he saw her eyes shining with a flame that his imagination immediately saw being kindled there at other times—who knows, even yesterday perhaps, or yet again tomorrow—kindled by someone else; when, having yielded to a purely physical desire for another woman, and remembering how many times before he had indulged such passions and had been able to lie to Françoise without ceasing to love her, he no longer thought it absurd to suppose that she also lied to him, and that to lie to him it was not even necessary for her not to love him, and that before knowing him she had thrown herself on others with the same ardor that now so excited him—and that seemed more terrible to him than the ardor that he inspired in her seemed sweet, because he saw it with the imagination which magnifies all things.

Then he tried to tell her that he had deceived her;

not with any idea of vengeance, nor from the need of making her suffer too, but with the hope that she would also tell him the truth in return, above all so as not to harbor those lies any longer, to expiate his sins of sensuality, since, in order to create an object for his jealousy, it seemed to him at times that it was his own deceit and his own sensuality he transferred to Françoise.

It was one evening while they were walking along the Champs Elysées that he tried to tell her he had been unfaithful. He was terrified to see her turn pale, sink powerless on a bench, and worse still when, gently and without anger, as he held out his hands to her, she pushed him away. For two days he thought he had lost her, or rather that he had found her again. But this involuntary proof, so striking and so pathetic, that she had just given him of her love, was not enough to satisfy Honoré. Even if he had acquired the impossible certitude that she had never given herself to anyone but to him, the unknown pain which had visited his heart the night that M. de Buivres had accompanied him to his door, not a kindred pain, or the memory of that pain, but that very pain itself, would not have ceased making him suffer even if he had been incontestably shown that it was without cause. Just as we still tremble in fear of the assassin of our dream even after we know that it was only an illusion, just as men still feel pain in the leg that has been amputated.

In vain during the day he would walk, wear himself

out with long rides on his horse, on his bicycle, with fencing; in vain he would meet Françoise, take her home and in the evening from her hands, her forehead, her eyes gather confidence, peace, the sweetness of honey, returning home still quieted and abounding in a fragrant provision of riches; yet hardly was he back in his apartment before his uneasiness would begin again, and he would quickly get into bed to try to fall asleep before his happiness should have altered, lying cautiously in the balm of that recent and fresh tenderness scarcely an hour old, to make it last through the night until the morning, intact and glorious like an Egyptian prince; but then inevitably would come creeping back into his thoughts Buivres' words, or any one of the innumerable images that had crowded his brain ever since, and he knew that there would be no more sleep for him that night. It would not yet have appeared, that image, but he would feel it hovering near him and, steeling himself against it, he would light his candle again, would read, would force himself without a pause to fill every corner of his brain and every instant with the sense of the phrases he was reading, so that the horrible image should not have a moment, should not find the tiniest loophole through which it could slip in.

But all at once he would find that it had entered, that it was there, and now he could no longer drive it away; the door of his attention, which he had been holding closed with all his might, had been opened by surprise. It had closed again, and he would spend the

entire night in that atrocious company; that night
like all the other nights he would not sleep a wink;
and again he had recourse to the bottle of bromide,
drank three spoonfuls, and, sure of sleeping, even
frightened at the thought that now he could not help
sleeping no matter what happened, began thinking of
Françoise again with terror, with despair, with hate.
Taking advantage of the fact that his liaison was not
known, he longed to make wagers with other men
about her virtue, make them test her virtue to see if
she would yield, try to discover something, to learn
everything; thought of hiding in her room (he remembered having, when younger, done such a thing)
to see. He would not betray himself, first of all on account of the others, since it was all his idea, his joke—
otherwise what a scandal! what indignation!—but,
above all, on her account, to see whether next day
when he asked her: "You haven't deceived me?" she
would reply: "Never!" with that same loving air. Perhaps she would admit everything, and had indeed
only succumbed because of all those ruses. And this
would act as a salutary operation, after which his love
would be cured of this disease that was killing him, as
the disease of a parasite kills a tree (he had only to
look at himself in the glass, feebly lighted by his
candle, to be sure of it). But no, for then that image
would keep coming back, how much more potent
than those of his imagination, striking his poor head
with what an incalculable force he did not even try
to conceive.

Then all at once he would think of her, of her
sweetness, her tenderness, her purity, and was ready to
weep at the outrage he had for an instant conceived
against her. The mere idea of proposing such a thing
to companions of debauch!

Soon he felt that generalized shiver, that fainting
sensation which precedes by a few moments the sleep
induced by bromide. Then, perceiving nothing, not a
dream, not a sensation, between his last thought and
the present one, he asked himself: "What! I haven't
gone to sleep yet?" But seeing that it was broad day-
light, he understood that for six hours he had been
wrapped in the unconscious sleep of bromide.

He waited for the shooting pains in his head to
abate a little, then he rose and tried in vain with cold
water and a vigorous walk to bring back some color to
his pale face, under his haggard eyes, afraid of horri-
fying Françoise by his appearance. On leaving the
house he entered a church, where, bent and weary,
with the last desperate effort of his sagging body that
wanted to be restored, rejuvenated, of his sick and
aging heart that wanted to be cured, of his mind, fore-
spent and harassed without respite, that wanted peace,
he prayed to God, God, from whom a month ago he
had begged the grace of loving Françoise forever,
prayed with the same force, ever with the force of that
love which, formerly sure of dying, asked to live, and
which now, afraid of living, begged to die; prayed to
be granted the grace of not loving Françoise any
longer, not to go on loving her forever, so that at last

he would be able to imagine her in the arms of someone else without suffering, since he could not help
forever imagining her in the arms of someone else.
And perhaps he would cease to imagine her like this
as soon as he could imagine it without pain.

Then he remembered how he had been afraid of
not loving her forever, how he had tried to engrave on
his memory, so that nothing could efface them, her
cheeks always lifted to his lips, her forehead, her
little hands, her grave eyes, her adored features.
Then, suddenly seeing them awakened from their
gentle calm by desire for another, he tried not to
think of them any longer, but would see them all the
more obstinately, her uplifted cheeks, her forehead,
her little hands—oh! those little hands, those too!—
her grave eyes, her hated features.

From that day, terrified himself in the beginning at
taking such a course, he never left Françoise for a
moment, spying on her life, accompanying her on all
her visits, following her when she went shopping,
waiting outside the shops for her. If he had thought
that he was preventing her by his conduct from actually deceiving him, he would, no doubt, have desisted
for fear of making himself loathsome in her eyes; but
she acquiesced with such joy at feeling him always
near her that, little by little, this joy became conta-
gious and slowly filled him with a confidence, a certitude that no material proof could have given him,
like those people suffering from hallucinations whom
sometimes one succeeds in curing by having them

touch the armchair or the living person occupying the place where they thought they saw a phantom, and thus chasing it from the real world, curing them by reality itself, which leaves no room for phantoms.

Honoré thus succeeded, by filling his mind with the actual occupations of all Françoise's days, in suppressing those shadowy and empty places where the evil spirits of jealousy and doubt lay in wait for him every evening. He began to sleep again, his sufferings were less frequent, of short duration, and if, when they came, he sent for her, a few moments of her presence sufficed to calm him for the night.

III

"The soul may be trusted to the end. That which is so beautiful and attractive as these relations must be succeeded and supplanted only by what is more beautiful, and so on forever."

—Emerson

The Salon of Madame Seaune, the former Princess de Galaise-Orlandes, of whom we have spoken in the first part of this story as Françoise, is still today one of the most fashionable *salons* of Paris. In a society where the title of duchess would not have distinguished her from so many others, her bourgeois name makes her stand out like a beauty-patch on a woman's cheek, and in exchange for the title she lost in marrying M. Seaune, she has acquired the prestige of having voluntarily renounced a glory akin to that which, for a refined imagination, exalts white peacocks, black swans, white violets and queens in captivity.

Madame Seaune has entertained extensively this season and the season before, but her salon was closed during the three preceding years, that is, during the years following the death of Honoré de Lenvres.

Honoré's friends, who were delighted to see him little by little regaining his former health and gaiety, now met him at all hours of the day with Madame Seaune, and attributed his recovery to this liaison, which they supposed of recent date.

It was hardly two months after this restoration that the accident of the Avenue du Bois-de-Boulogne occurred in which he had both legs broken by a runaway horse. The accident took place the first Tuesday in May; on Sunday peritonitis set in. Honoré received the last sacraments Monday, and died that same Monday at six o'clock in the evening. But from Tuesday, the day of the accident, to Sunday night, he alone knew there was no hope. Tuesday, toward six o'clock, he asked to be left alone, but requested that the cards of all those who had come to inquire be brought to him.

The same morning, not eight hours before, he had been walking down the Avenue du Bois-de-Boulogne. He had breathed and exhaled by turn in the air mixed with wind and sun, had recognized in the depths of women's eyes that followed admiringly his fleeting grace, an instant lost in a turn of his own capricious gaiety, easily caught again and quickly outstripped in the midst of the galloping and steaming horses, had relished in the coolness of his mouth, ravenous and refreshed by the delicious air, the profound joy embellishing life that morning, with sun, with shadows, sky, stones, the eastern wind, and trees; trees as majestic as men erect, as relaxed as women asleep in all their dazzling immobility.

At a certain moment he had glanced at his watch, had retraced his steps and then . . . then it had happened. In a second the horse he had not seen had broken both his legs. It did not seem to him that that particular second must inevitably have been like that. At that very second he might have been a little farther away, a little nearer, or the horse might have deviated a little, or it might have rained and he would have gone home before; or if he had not looked at his watch he would not have retraced his steps and would have continued his walk to the cascade. But yet this thing which so easily might not have been, that he could for a moment pretend was nothing but a dream, this thing was something real, was now a part of his life, and nothing he could do would change it. He had two broken legs and a bruised body. Oh! the accident in itself was nothing so extraordinary. He remembered that not eight days before, during a dinner at Doctor S . . .'s, they were speaking of C . . ., who had been hurt in exactly the same way by a runaway horse. The doctor, being asked about C . . .'s condition, said, "It is extremely grave." Honoré had insisted, questioned him about the injury, and the doctor had replied with an important, pedantic and melancholy air, "But it is not only the injury itself; it is all the attendant circumstances combined. His sons are worrying him; his business is not what it was; the attacks in the newspaper have been a terrible blow to him. I wish I were wrong, but his condition is critical." Having said this, the doctor felt himself, on the contrary, to be in excellent health, healthier, more intelligent, more highly thought of than ever, and Honoré, knowing that Françoise loved him more and more, that the world had accepted their liaison, not only respecting their happiness but also the nobility of Françoise's character; and finally, the wife of Doctor S . . ., touched to think of the miserable and abandoned death of C . . . (but never allowing herself, for the sake of her health and that of her children, to dwell on tragic events or to go to funerals), each one repeated for the last time, "Poor C . . .; his condition is critical," while they swallowed another glass of champagne, relishing the pleasure it gave them and thinking that their own "condition" was excellent.

But this was not at all the same thing. Honoré felt himself overwhelmed by the thought of his misfortune, as he had often been at the thought of other people's misfortunes, but now he found it impossible to regain his inner equilibrium. He felt slipping beneath his feet that solid ground of good health on which flourish all our lofty resolutions and our most gracious joys, just as oaks and violets have their roots

in the black, moist earth; and he kept stumbling
around blindly trying to find himself. Speaking of
C . . . at that dinner, which he now recalled, the doctor had said, "Even before the accident and after the
attacks in the papers, meeting C . . ., I thought then
how yellow he looked, how hollow-eyed, the look of a
very sick man!" And the doctor had passed his hand,
a clever hand famous for its beauty, over his sleek and
rosy cheek, down his fine, silky and well-kept beard,
and everyone there had thought with pleasure of his
own blooming looks, like a proprietor who stops to
observe with satisfaction one of his tenants, still
young, satisfied and rich. Now Honoré, looking at
himself in the glass, was terrified by his "yellow face,"
his "look of a very sick man!" And immediately the
thought that the doctor would make the same remarks about him that he had made about C . . ., and
with the same indifference, terrified him. Even those
who came to him full of pity would turn quickly away
as from something inimical to themselves; would end
up by obeying the protestations of their healthiness
and of their desire to live and be happy. Then his
thought turned to Françoise and, letting his shoulders
droop, bowing his head in spite of himself, as though
the commandment of God had appeared before him,
he understood with an infinite and submissive sadness that he must give her up. He had the sensation of
the humility of his body bent with his child's weakness, his sick man's resignation, before this enormous
grief, and he pitied himself just as, when a child at

the very beginning of his life, he had so often regarded himself with a tender compassion, and he could have wept.

Someone knocked. They had brought him the cards as he had requested. He knew very well that people would send to inquire about him, for he was aware that his accident was serious, but he had never dreamed that there would be so many cards, and he was terrified to see how many people had called who knew him only slightly and who would never disturb themselves except for a wedding or a funeral. It was a mountain of cards, and the concierge had to carry them carefully to keep them from falling off the large tray they overflowed. But all at once, when he had them beside him, all these cards, this mountain seemed such a very little thing, really absurdly little, smaller, much smaller than the chair or the chimney. And he was still more terrified that it was so little, and he felt so alone that, to divert his attention, he began to read the names; one card, two cards, a third card— ah! he trembled and looked again: "Comte François de Gouvres." Yet he might have known that M. de Gouvres would come to inquire, but it had been so long since he had thought of him, and immediately the phrase of de Buivres: *"There was someone there tonight who must have had quite an affair with her. It was François de Gouvres; he says she is certainly passionate but has a horrible body, and he didn't go on,"* came back to him, and feeling all his former suffering which from the depth of his consciousness rose again to the surface, he said to himself: "Now I am glad there is no hope. Not to die, to remain riveted here, and for years, all the time that she would not be with me, a large part of the day, all night long, imagining her with someone else! And it wouldn't be because of a diseased imagination then that I should see her like that, it would really be like that. How could she go on loving me? Without legs!" Suddenly he paused. "And if I die—after me?"

She was thirty. He skipped over the time, more or less long, during which she would remember him, be faithful to him. But a moment would come ... *"she is passionate ... ,"* he says. "I want to live, I want to live and I want to walk, I want to follow her everywhere, I want to be handsome, I want her to love me!"

Just then he was frightened to hear his breathing, it was hissing terribly, and he felt a pain in his side; his chest seemed to be touching his back, he could not breathe freely; he tried to draw a deep breath and was unable to. With each respiration he felt himself breathing, but not breathing enough. The doctor came. He was suffering from a slight nervous attack of asthma; the doctor left. Honoré was disappointed; he would have preferred it to have been something serious, to be pitied. For he knew very well that if this wasn't serious, something else was, and that he was going to die. Now he remembered all the physical sufferings of his whole life, he was disconsolate; never had those who loved him the most ever pitied him because of his nerves. During those terrible months after that night with Buivres when at seven o'clock in the morning, after having walked all night, his brother, who might at the most lie awake for a quarter of an hour the nights after too copious a dinner, said to him, "You observe yourself too much; I too have nights when I don't sleep. And besides, one thinks one doesn't sleep, but one always sleeps a little."

It is true that he observed himself too much; in the background of his life he was always observing death which was never completely absent, and without altogether destroying his life, undermined it now here, now there. His asthma grew worse; he could not get his breath; his whole chest was making painful efforts to breathe. And he felt the veil that hides life, death which is within us, being lifted, and perceived what a terrible thing it is to breathe, to live.

Then he found himself thinking of the moment when she would be consoled, and after that . . . who would it be? And the veiled uncertainty of the event, together with its inevitability, made him mad with jealousy. Living, he would be able to prevent it, but he could not live, and so? She would tell him that she would enter a convent. Then, after his death, would change her mind. No! He preferred not to be doubly deceived, he preferred to know. Who? Gouvres, Alériouvre, Buivres, Breyves? Gritting his teeth he saw them all, he felt a furious rebellion which must have contorted his face at that moment. He

quieted himself. No, it mustn't be one of those, not
a mere playboy, it must be a man who really loves
her. Why shouldn't I want him to be a playboy? How
silly of me to ask; it's only natural. Because I really
love her, because I want her to be happy— No, it isn't
that, it's because I don't want her senses to be stirred,
I don't want anyone to give her more pleasure than
I have given her, give her any pleasure at all. I want
him to give her happiness, I want him to give
her love, but I don't want anyone to give her
pleasure. I am jealous of the other man's pleasure, I
am jealous of her pleasure. I should not be jealous
of their love. She must get married, she must choose
carefully. . . . But it will be sad just the same.

Then one of his little boy exigencies came back to
him, of the little boy he was at seven when he went to
bed every night at eight o'clock. The nights when his
mother, instead of staying in her room, which was
next to his, until twelve o'clock and then going to
bed, had to go to some affair at eleven and until then
would be busy dressing, he used to beg her to dress
before dinner and to go away—anywhere, because he
could not endure the idea that, while he was trying to
sleep, anyone was preparing for a party, preparing to
go out. And to please him and to quiet him, his
mother, all dressed for the evening in low neck gown
at eight o'clock, would come to kiss him good night
and then would go to stay with a friend until the
hour of the ball. And only in this way, grieved but

calm, on those sad days when his mother was going to a ball, could he get to sleep.

Now the same prayer he had made to his mother, the same prayer to Françoise rose to his lips. He would have liked to ask her to marry at once, that she would be ready, so that he might fall asleep forever, desolate but calm, and no longer troubled by the thought of what might happen after he was asleep.

During the days that followed he tried to talk to Françoise, but like the doctor himself, she did not believe he was dying and rejected with gentle but inflexible firmness Honoré's proposal.

They were so accustomed to telling each other the truth that they told the truth, each of them, even if it hurt the other, as though at bottom, at the bottom of their nervous and sensitive being which needed such gentle treatment, they had felt the presence of a God, superior and indifferent to all those precautions suitable only for children, and who demanded the truth, and to whom the truth was due. And toward this God who was at the bottom of Françoise, Honoré, and toward this God who was at the bottom of Honoré, Françoise, had always felt duties before which the desire not to hurt, not to offend the other, those honest lies of tenderness and pity, gave way.

Moreover, when Françoise said to Honoré that he was going to live, he felt that she really believed it and gradually persuaded himself to believe it too:

If I am to die, I shall not be jealous after I am dead; but until I am dead? As long as my body is alive, yes! But since I am only jealous of her pleasure, since it is my body that is jealous, since what makes me jealous is not her heart, not her happiness, which is what I desire for her from the person most capable of making her happy, when my body no longer counts, when the soul has got the better of it, when I shall, little by little, have become detached from material things, as I did once before when I was very ill, when I no longer madly desire her body and love her soul as much, then I shall not be jealous any more. Then I shall truly love her. I cannot very well conceive what that will be like while my body is still so full of life and rebellion, but I can imagine it faintly when I think of those hours when, my hand in her hand, I found in an infinite tenderness, and entirely free from desire, the appeasement of my sufferings and my jealousy. I shall feel great sorrow in leaving her, but the kind of sorrow that formerly brought me closer to myself, that brought an angel to console me, that sorrow which revealed to me the mysterious friend of evil days, my own soul, that calm sorrow, thanks to which I shall feel more worthy to appear before God, and not that horrible disease which made me suffer for so long without uplifting my heart, like a physical pain that stabs, degrades, diminishes. Together with my body, with the desire of my body, I shall be delivered from it too. Yes, but until then, what will become of me? Weaker, less able than ever to resist, hampered by my two broken legs when longing to rush to her to make sure she is not where I dreamed she was, I shall have to sit there unable to move, laughed at by everyone who can "make her" without a qualm, right under the eyes of the cripple they no longer fear.

The night of Sunday to Monday he dreamed he was suffocating, felt an enormous weight on his chest. He begged for mercy, had no longer strength enough to move all that weight, could not understand his feeling that it had all been like this for a long time. He could not endure it another moment; he was suffocating. Suddenly he felt himself relieved of this terrible burden that was disappearing, disappearing—felt himself relieved of it forever. And he said to himself: "I am dead."

And looking up, he saw above him what had weighed on him, been suffocating him so long; at first he thought that it was the image of de Gouvres, then that it was only his suspicions, then his desires, then his impatient waitings on those mornings in the past when he would cry out for the moment to arrive when he should see Françoise, then the thought of Françoise. At every moment it took a different form; like a cloud, it grew bigger and bigger, and now he could not understand how this thing that he knew to be as big as the world could have rested on him, on his body, his little weak man's body, on his poor irresolute heart, and how it had not crushed him. And then he knew that it *had* crushed him, and that he had all this time been nothing but a crushed man. And this immense thing which had weighed on his chest with the force of the whole world, he now realized that it was his love.

Then he repeated: "Nothing but a crushed man!" and he remembered at the moment the horse had knocked him down he had thought, "I shall be crushed"; he remembered his walk, remembered that he was to have had luncheon with Françoise, and then, in this roundabout way, the thought of his love returned to him. And he asked himself: "Was it my love that weighed on me? And if not my love, what was it? My character, perhaps? Myself? Or was it Life?" Then he thought: "No, when I die I shall not be delivered of my love but of my carnal desires, my mortal envy, of my jealousy." Then he said: "My God, let that hour come, let it come quickly, my God, so that I may know the perfect love at last."

Sunday night peritonitis set in; Monday morning about ten o'clock his fever rose; he wanted Françoise, called for her, his eyes blazing: "I want your eyes to shine too, I want to give you pleasure as never before . . . I want to . . . until it hurts." Then suddenly he grew pale with rage. "I know why you don't want to, I know very well what you've been having done to you this morning, and where, and by whom, and I know that he wanted to send for me, hide me behind the door because then I could see you but would not be able to throw myself on you since I haven't any legs, couldn't stop you, and because you would have had all the more pleasure seeing me there all the time. He knows very well what to do to give you pleasure, but I'll kill him first, I'll kill you too, and even before, I'll kill myself. You see! I've killed myself!" And he fell back lifeless on the pillows.

Little by little he grew calmer and went on trying to think of someone she could marry after his death, but there were always those images which he brushed aside, that of François de Gouvres, that of Buivres, which tortured him, kept coming back.

At noon he received the last sacraments. The doctor said he would not live through the afternoon. His strength was rapidly failing, he could take no nourishment, could hardly hear. His mind remained clear, and without saying anything, so as not to hurt Françoise, who, he could see, was overcome with grief, he thought of her as she would be after he knew nothing more, knew nothing more about her, when it would be impossible for her to go on loving him any longer.

The names that he had repeated mechanically only that morning began filing through his mind again, while his eyes followed a fly that came close to his finger as though to light on it, then flew away, came again without, however, touching it; and then, reviving his attention that had lapsed for a moment, as the name of François de Gouvres returned, and he thought to himself that it was indeed very possible that Gouvres would possess her, he was at the same time thinking: "Is that fly going to light on the sheet? No, not yet," then brusquely rousing himself: "What!

Are the two things of the same importance to me? Is Gouvres going to possess Françoise, is the fly going to light on the sheet? Oh, possessing Françoise is a little more important." But the precision with which he saw the difference that separated these two events showed him that the one did not touch him much more than the other. And he said to himself: "To think it makes so little difference to me! How sad it is!" Then he noticed that he said: "How sad it is," only through force of habit and that, having completely changed, he was not in the least sad that he had changed. His lips parted in a vague smile. "So this," he said, "is my pure love for Françoise. I am no longer jealous, I must be very near to death; but what does it matter, since in order for me to feel true love for Françoise, it had to be."

But then, raising his eyes, he saw Françoise kneeling in the midst of the servants, the doctor, two old relatives, who were all praying around his bed. And he noticed that the love, free of all selfishness, of all sensuality, that he had dreamed would be so sweet, so vast and so divine when it came to him, cherished, now that it had come, the old relatives, the servants, even the doctor as tenderly as Françoise, and that already feeling for her the same love as for all creatures with whom his kindred soul united him, he had no longer any other love for her. And this could not even sadden him now, so completely had all exclusive love for her, even the idea of a preference for her, disappeared.

Weeping at the foot of his bed, she murmured the loveliest of their former words: "My country, my brother." But having neither the desire nor the force to undeceive her, he only smiled and thought that his "country" was no longer in Françoise but in the sky and throughout the entire earth. In his heart he whispered, "My brothers," and if he looked at her more than at the others it was only out of pity, because of the flood of tears she shed before his eyes; his eyes that soon would close and that could no longer weep. But he did not love her more than he loved the doctor, the old relatives, the servants, and not differently. And this was the end of his jealousy.

Grafton Classics

Honoré de Balzac
Droll Stories   £2.95 ☐

Emile Zola
The Beast in Man   £2.95 ☐
The Kill   £2.95 ☐
Restless House   £3.50 ☐

Lion Feuchtwanger
Jew Süss   £3.95 ☐

Richard Jefferies
Greene Ferne Farm   £2.50 ☐

Charles Dickens
David Copperfield   £3.95 ☐

To order direct from the publisher just tick the titles you want
and fill in the order form.   **GF984**

The world's greatest novelists now available in paperback from Grafton Books

Simon Raven
'Alms for Oblivion' Series

Fielding Gray	£1.95	☐
Sound the Retreat	£1.95	☐
The Sabre Squadron	£1.95	☐
The Rich Pay Late	£1.95	☐
Friends in Low Places	£1.95	☐
The Judas Boy	£1.95	☐
Places Where They Sing	£1.95	☐
Come Like Shadows	£1.95	☐
Bring Forth the Body	£1.95	☐
The Survivors	£1.95	☐

'First Born of Egypt' Series

Morning Star	£2.50	☐
The Face of the Waters	£3.50	☐

Paul Scott
The Raj Quartet

The Jewel in the Crown	£2.95	☐
The Day of the Scorpion	£2.95	☐
The Towers of Silence	£2.95	☐
A Division of the Spoils	£2.95	☐

Other Titles

The Bender	£2.50	☐
The Corrida at San Feliu	£2.50	☐
A Male Child	£2.50	☐
The Alien Sky	£2.50	☐
The Chinese Love Pavilion	£2.95	☐
The Mark of the Warrior	£2.50	☐
Johnnie Sahib	£2.50	☐
The Birds of Paradise	£2.50	☐
Staying On	£2.95	☐

To order direct from the publisher just tick the titles you want
and fill in the order form.   **GF381**